Sarah Michaels—Her first marriage was a disaster. The only good thing that came out of it was her son. But life's not easy for Sarah—raising a child alone, working full-time, running a household, paying her bills. She copes, though. Her worst fear is that, without a husband, she can't provide the kind of male companionship an eight-year-old boy needs. That's why she signed up with Befriend an Island Child....

Farrell Michaels, Jr.—He's crazy about soccer, hates having his grammar corrected and would rather be called Mike. He knows his mom loves him—but he can't help wanting to do "guy things." Can't help wanting a dad....

Gabe Parker—He volunteers with Befriend an Island Child because he believes in children, believes in taking responsibility for his community. It takes Gabe a while to understand why Sarah reacts to him with such mistrust. But as he and young Mike grow closer—and as he falls in love with Sarah—he's determined not to let the ghost of a dead marriage come between them.

Dear Reader,

Children have a way of blending innocence with wisdom, and the result is often the kind of naked honesty we adults avoid. Not only do these innocents get away with saying absolutely outrageous things, but we love them for it! "Out of the mouths of babes" come some amazing truths.

Children beguile and charm their way into our hearts, as no other creature can. (Except maybe a puppy. But children and puppies go together, don't they?) Since I worked for a number of years as a secretary to three pediatricians and later in an elementary school office, you might think I wouldn't be so easily beguiled anymore. You'd be wrong! Because even now I'm still captivated by wide eyes, gap-toothed grins and childish giggles. It doesn't matter whether it's a little girl with a dirty face and skinned knees or a mischievous freckle-faced boy.

In the case of *Island Child*, it's a freckle-faced boy doing the captivating. Much as I love eight-year-old Mike, I've tried not to let him take over here. This is really his mother Sarah's story. I have met a number of remarkable single mothers who, like Sarah, deal with their little charmers on a twenty-four-hour-a-day basis. However, Mike is such a scamp, I thought Sarah needed help—which I provided in the form of Gabe Parker, adult male. At first, Sarah didn't appreciate my interference. But later... Well, you know, some rascally boys grow up to become pretty beguiling men!

Sincerely,

Roz Denny

P.S. I love hearing from readers. You can reach me at
3520 Knickerbocker #224, San Angelo, Texas 76904

ISLAND CHILD

Roz Denny

Harlequin Books

TORONTO • NEW YORK • LONDON
AMSTERDAM • PARIS • SYDNEY • HAMBURG
STOCKHOLM • ATHENS • TOKYO • MILAN
MADRID • WARSAW • BUDAPEST • AUCKLAND

ISBN 0-373-03320-6

ISLAND CHILD

This edition published by arrangement with Harlequin Enterprises B. V.

Printed in U.S.A.

CHAPTER ONE

"PHEW! WHAT A DAY. What a *week!* Where are those five-o'clock trade winds when we need them?"

Sarah Michaels drummed her fingers on the steering wheel and offered her best friend a look of sympathy. But as Mitzi was getting into the car, Sarah glimpsed a toy airplane in the passenger seat—where Mitzi was about to sit without looking. Her son must have left it after their midmorning trip to the dentist.

Sarah dove for it. *Success!* She grimaced and tossed it into the back. Only slightly winded from the effort, she picked up the conversation, never missing a beat. "Oahu with record spring heat, and my car's air conditioner on the fritz. Murphy's Law," she said wryly. "You know, Mitzi, I wouldn't blame you if you didn't pay a cent toward gas this month. I'm only hoping I can swing fixing it next payday." Sighing, she lifted a heavy fall of mink-brown hair from her neck and waited while her friend buckled up.

"Why won't you let me lend you the money?" Mitzi Kealoha asked as she unsheathed a lacy ivory fan.

"It's not your problem, Mitzi." Sarah shook her hair loose and met the other woman's gaze squarely, even though her fingers tightened imperceptibly on the wheel. "Look at you. Nobody in this day and age carries a fan."

"So I'm a traditionalist. I swear, Sarah, you're the most stubborn woman I know."

"I prefer to think of it as independent. Don't forget, I'm in this mess because someone we know lived beyond his means."

Mitzi fanned herself furiously. "Farrell Michaels hoodwinked a lot of people. Borrowing from me wouldn't be like second-mortgaging your house. If you didn't drive me to and from work every day, I'd have to take the bus. At least let me call my cousin with the garage. He'll give you a good deal." Moments later she nudged Sarah and giggled. "Did you see the once-over we got from the hunk loading his surfboard?" She peeked over the fluted ivory and batted her eyelashes. "It's the fan. I bet he thinks we're rich and mysterious."

"In this beat-up old junker? You nut." Sarah shook her head and her soft brown eyes twinkled. "Anybody but a surfer, and I'd stop to warn the poor devil that you're married to the island's top college-wrestling coach."

"Not all surfers are like those jerks your ex hung out with, Sarah." Mitzi closed her fan. "Osamu and I know what a struggle you've had since Farrell cleaned out your bank account and sailed off into the sunset with that bimbo. We want to help. What else are friends for?"

Sarah navigated the turn into Mitzi's driveway. "You and Osamu do too much now. I didn't just fall off a turnip wagon, you know. There's the small matter of you two inviting little Farrell and me to dinner at the end of every month. And I fight your mom to pay for the days she keeps him before or after school—never mind all those months I took night classes."

Mitzi waved a hand. "We love being needed."

Not wanting to get emotional, Sarah turned to stare out at the busy highway. Adroitly she changed the subject. "I remember when we had a definite tourist season here. Now it's year-round. Do you think traffic on the mainland is better?"

Mitzi gave a start. "Sarah, you wouldn't leave Oahu? This is home."

Sarah shrugged. "I've considered it. Maybe if we got completely away from here, Farrell would be happier."

"He'd be happier if you called him Mike."

"I do—when I remember. But that's only the tip of the iceberg."

"What's this mood really about, Sarah? Not just a faulty air conditioner. Is Farrell, Sr. causing trouble?"

"Other than being his normal eight months' delinquent on child support?" Sarah motioned toward the overcrowded beach and sighed. "You know, I can't remember my last vacation. Oh, don't listen to me." She wrinkled her nose. "Maybe I'm going through midlife crisis."

"At thirty?" her companion scoffed.

"My son isn't even nine yet," Sarah lamented, "and already I can't cope."

"What? This from the woman who recites child-care experts word for word?"

"Theory and practice are two different things, I've discovered." A sad expression flitted across Sarah's face. "So many times I find myself wondering how a man—a real father—would handle things."

"Farrell was never a real father. Surely this isn't about wanting him back?"

"Not on your life."

"Good!" Mitzi exploded. "After the way that louse squandered everything your father left you on a yacht! He'd be some dandy role model for a boy, living with that beach bunny young enough to be his daughter."

"He never wanted children. Having a baby was my idea. I can't believe I was so naive. I actually thought it might change him—keep him home more."

"We were all wrong. When you were dating, he was different. Charming. He *sounded* like he wanted a wife, family, the whole bit. So you can't tell me he didn't know how babies are made."

Sarah colored. "He left precautions up to me."

"Farrell Michaels wanted the convenience of marriage, but none of the responsibilities. Not all men are like that, Sarah. It's been five years. Time to get out where you'll meet some nice men."

"Mitzi, we've had this discussion before."

"I hate to be blunt, but Mike talks a lot about wanting a father. When my brothers were his age, our dad spent hours with them. What do your child-care experts say?"

"Of course they say all boys need a man to emulate at some point in their formative years." Sarah gave a troubled shrug.

"You know Osamu would fill in more if he wasn't out of town with the team so much." Mitzi touched Sarah's arm. "That's the big reason we haven't started a family of our own yet."

Sarah let a smile chase her moodiness away as she said her goodbyes.

Mitzi was half out the door when she paused. "Hey, that reminds me—did you ever get in touch with that group Osamu told you about? What's it called? Befriend Our Kids or something?"

Sarah's eyes widened. "Befriend an Island Child. Funny you should mention them. When Osamu first gave me the brochure, I filled out the application and we were put on a waiting list. Yesterday the director called to say one of the children in the program just moved to the mainland. Apparently that freed up a man they've already screened and approved." She gripped the wheel. "I didn't commit myself. I mean, what kind of men volunteer?"

"Entrepreneurs. Local men who like kids. Call them," Mitzi urged. "Osamu said several members in his Rotary are involved in the program."

Sarah looked unsure. "If only Harvey and Farrell—" she stopped and corrected herself. "I mean Mike. I wish those two could communicate."

"Harvey Denton?" Mitzi snorted. "Who could communicate with that pompous ass? What you see in such a stuffed shirt is beyond me."

"We both enjoy opera and theater. Besides, who else asks me out?"

"I'd be the last to begrudge you an outing. But Harvey is so…so…" Mitzi didn't finish what she'd been about to say. "You need to hang loose, Sarah."

"Hang loose, indeed!" Sarah shooed Mitzi from the car. "That was Farrell's philosophy. It's how he ran through a trust fund set up by his grandfather and why his family disowned him—along with any kids he might have. I'm not a party girl, Mitzi. I never will be. Anyway, I hate to rush you, but I need to stop at the grocery store before I go home. Mike's soccer coach goes right by the house tonight, so he's dropping him off after practice. He doesn't like it if parents aren't there to meet their kids."

"So tell him to try being a single mom."

"He has a big family. Tuesday, he lectured me about parenting responsibilities." Sarah made a face. "Me! Can you believe it?"

Mitzi shook her head. "Point taken. I'll get off my soapbox now. See you tomorrow. Promise me you'll think about calling that agency back. Could be the friend they assign Mike will pick him up sometimes from soccer. Either you find some time for yourself or you're gonna crack, woman."

When Sarah didn't respond, Mitzi poked her head back inside the car. "Sam's out of town for two weeks. You wanna take Mike out for pizza, Friday? My treat," she added hastily.

"Sounds great, but you'll have to suffer a soccer game first. And I'll pay our share of the pizza." Sarah tugged the door out of Mitzi's hands, then backed out before her friend could argue. She narrowly missed a bright Jeep filled with tourists. She had to get a grip. This was ridiculous.

Except that melancholy descended again before she reached the freeway. She *knew* Farrell Sr. was a louse, darn it. But knowing didn't necessarily make it easier to accept. At times she still felt like a failure because of his leaving. Lord knew she'd given all she could to make the marriage work. She'd never intended her son to be an only child, either. Her own youth, lost in caring for an invalid mother while her father traveled with the military, was a big reason she wanted Mike's childhood to be enjoyable.

Her private musings were cut short when a van, loaded down with jet-skis and surfboards, crowded in front of her.

Forced to brake suddenly, Sarah leaned on her horn and muttered an oath under her breath. She could write a book about lordly muscle-bound surfers and their sex-kitten girlfriends. Her home had been overrun with them for the whole of her marriage. And that included air-headed DeeDee Forbes, who had blithely sailed away with Farrell.

Suddenly weary of reminiscing, Sarah rolled her head around her shoulders, trying to relax. That last thought had been unworthy of her. Lately it seemed her tolerance for even little annoyances was zilch. For instance, she had no patience for this bumper-to-bumper traffic. Sighing, she checked her watch to see if she still had time to stop for groceries. Mike knew where she kept the extra house key, but she did always try to beat him home. The books all said how important it was to spend time listening to your child when he came in from school.

Well, eating's important too, she thought as she whipped into a parking space outside the store. No matter how carefully she shopped, it seemed they were always out of milk and bread.

She dashed inside and down the familiar aisles at top speed. Then she had to wait in line at the checkout. Two young men in front of her were involved in surfing talk. It was difficult not to overhear. Surf was up at Makaha and they were as impatient as she was to get through the line.

It didn't take Sarah long to see that those two had the same preoccupation with waves that her former husband had. She tried blocking out their words—which were mostly about getting into the curl of the Banzai. The Banzai Pipeline was a surfer's ultimate dream.

Or obsession, as in Farrell's case, Sarah recalled. If she lived to be a hundred, she'd never understand how grown men could put surfing ahead of everything and everyone else, including family. Sadly, Farrell hadn't been alone in that respect, either. Was she way off base to want a well-balanced male in her son's life?

It was a moment before Sarah realized one of the two young men was attempting to flirt with her. She pressed her lips into a tight line and looked away from the tanned muscles he was showing off. Honestly. Did surfer types think all women panted after their half-naked bodies?

"Hey, baby," the dark-haired fellow murmured, "wanna hang loose? Surf's up. It's party time. Sun and fun." He winked.

Sarah was set to tell him what he could do with his brand of fun, except that the line moved and it was their turn at the register. Heavens, it wasn't like her to get into verbal battles with perfect strangers. Maybe she really *was* undergoing some sort of midlife crisis.

The men forgot about her as they paid for their purchases. Hot dogs, chips and beer. Standard fare for beach parties. She hadn't stocked any of those items in years. How unfair to Mike, she suddenly realized, making a mental note to add picnic supplies to her next grocery list. She watched the young men clowning around as they left and again resented Farrell for having stolen whatever carefree piece of herself there might once have been.

Her resentment wilted, however, under the force of the late-afternoon sun as she walked out to her car. By the time she arrived home, Sarah was completely drained of energy. Coach had said five-thirty on the dot, and she'd made it with one minute to spare.

But the coach was late. As six o'clock approached, Sarah worried that something might have happened. She called the school. No answer. Between storing her groceries and dumping two cans of stew into a pot to simmer, she almost wore a path to the window. Which was another thing Mitzi scolded her about—worrying. But how did one *not* worry, she wanted to know, when there was no one else to care?

Unable to help herself, she was heading for another quick peek out the front window when the coach's consumptive van pulled into her long driveway. Relieved, Sarah hurried to open the door. Her heart swelled as she watched the pride of her life scramble from the van and meander toward the house, aimlessly kicking his soccer ball. Sunlight filtered through his golden curls, turning the outer edges flaxen. A lump rose in her throat and Sarah almost felt sorry for her ex-husband—that he was missing the joys of parenting.

Not that parenting was *always* joyful. Like now... As she caught sight of heavy grass stains covering both her son's knees. And the ragged tear in the pocket of his brand-new shirt. Sarah rubbed her temples, hating when dollars and cents got in the way of simply loving him.

Swallowing any reference she might have made about the condition of her son's clothes, she called out a greeting. "Hi, Mike." The nickname she tried to use, but sometimes forgot, came out sounding a bit choked—enough so that he was taken off guard and lost his ball in the bushes.

"Mom?" He retrieved the ball, then, at the foot of the steps, shaded his eyes to study her.

"Did you have a good practice?" She acted nonchalant.

"Naw, we did lousy. Coach said!" He wiggled through the door past her and screwed up his face, showing white teeth with several gaps between them. They were responsible for a slight lisp, and just last week his teacher had suggested speech therapy. But Sarah insisted on waiting until his permanent teeth grew in. If that didn't take care of the problem...well, she'd just have to handle it, along with everything else. The dentist was hopeful—but not certain. A sigh welled up before she could stifle it.

"Guess what, Mom?" Mike shouted from the kitchen. "Our first workout this Friday is against the Dolphins. They're tough. But Coach said if we practice, we can cream 'em."

Sarah rolled her eyes and picked up his jacket, which had slid from the chair where he'd aimed it and missed. She'd been hearing all these "Coach said" tidbits since practice started a week ago. But except for the added expense of fees, uniform deposit and ball, she didn't really mind. Mike seemed happier, and she'd manage. She always had. Sneaking up behind him, Sarah dropped a quick kiss on his ear. "Hey, boyo, Mitzi's coming with me to watch you play on Friday, so you better be good."

He wiped her kiss away and asked eagerly, "Sam, too?"

Sarah bit her lip. "Afraid not. Osamu will be out of town. He has students in competition. Maybe he'll make your first league game." She hated disappointing Mike, but it couldn't be helped.

"Guess so," he muttered. "It's good you and Aunt Mitzi are gonna watch this one, but I hope Sam can come when I really play." He frowned. "Today Coach said I need more work on kicking. Too bad Sam isn't gonna be around this weekend. Most of the guys have a dad to kick the ball around with them."

Sarah busied herself stirring the stew. She jumped when some splashed on her blouse. "Uh, maybe I can squeeze in some time Sunday afternoon. Would you like to take your soccer ball and a picnic lunch to the park near Fort De Russy? We haven't done that before."

"Aw, Mom!" He made a face. "What if any of the guys see me? I mean, you're my *mom!* They'd think I was a sissy or something. I'll wait for Sam."

Sarah recognized some of her own stubbornness in the set of his chin, and yet she resented the social conditioning that made life difficult for single mothers—especially mothers of boys. She slapped a lid on the stew.

Mike sniffed the air. "What's for dinner?"

"I wondered when you'd get around to the really important stuff. Canned stew. With fresh fruit for dessert," she added, wondering guiltily about the nutritional content of their main course. "Mike, I'm bushed and I still have laundry."

"Yuck! We always have stew. You're tired too much. When Todd Wilson's mom is tired, they go out for hamburgers. Why don't we do that?"

Sarah handed him the bowls. "I explained that property taxes went up. Plus, I have to save enough money to fix the car air conditioner. The heat wears me out, Mike." Her eyes begged for his understanding.

"Why don't you just buy a new car? The Clines bought one. It's bright red. Real neat. I saw Jim get out of it at school this morning."

"Really?" Sarah only knew Mrs. Cline through PTA. She'd been the most vocal mother at the first parent soccer meeting.

"Yep." He kicked at the ball and watched it smack against the underside of the table, displacing flatware.

Sarah straightened the forks and spoons. "I imagine the Clines both have good jobs."

Mike hooted. "Jim's mom stays home and bakes brownies. His dad works. Jim says he does vestments or something."

"Investments," Sarah corrected, taking his ball away. "That means people give him money and he knows where to put it to make more."

"Why don't you give him some money? Then we could buy a new car, too." He gave her an expectant look and stopped trying to retrieve the ball she'd placed out of his reach on top of the refrigerator.

"I wish I could." She laughed. "Go wash up. Put that dirty shirt in the laundry and get a clean one from your closet." She ruffled his hair affectionately and softened her tone. "Listen, Mike. Investing isn't all that easy. It takes money to get started, and right now we don't have a penny to spare."

Sarah steeled herself for the type of outburst she'd dealt with lately whenever she'd refused something he wanted because money was tight. But this time her son remained silent. His shoulders sagged and he trudged out, unbuttoning his shirt as he went. Sarah didn't know which was worse, his temper or this dejection.

When it came time to eat, neither of them showed much interest in the stew. Sarah ate a bite now and then between sorting bills. She wondered which ones could be juggled to work in the car repair.

Mike picked at his food and kicked his feet rhythmically against the table leg. He was about to get a warning when the telephone rang. Sarah rose to answer it, hurrying into the hall.

"Mrs Michaels?" a deep voice queried.

"Yes," she said hesitantly, not recognizing the caller. For no apparent reason, a chill raised goose bumps on her arms. She anchored the phone against her shoulder and rubbed them away.

"My name is Gabe Parker."

Sarah waited for him to say more, but the line merely crackled with static. "Yes?" This time her tone was sharp. Her meat was getting cold and she had at least three loads of laundry to do before calling it a night. "Whatever you're selling, Mr. Parker, I'm not buying. To put it bluntly, I'm broke."

He laughed, and Sarah retorted, "If my lack of funds amuses you, Mr. Parker, I assume you're not a bill collector."

"No ma'am, I'm not." His tone was suddenly brisk. "It was my understanding that Bill Evans, from Befriend an Island Child, called you about me. I've been assigned to your son, Mrs. Michaels, and as I'm in the area, I was wondering if I could drop by for a few minutes to get acquainted?"

Sarah's stomach bottomed out. Yes, she remembered now. Mr. Evans *had* told her about Gabe Parker. She'd only half listened, not believing anything would come of it. From the kitchen, she could hear Mike asking who was on the phone. She clutched the receiver until her fingers ached, not knowing how to answer either her son or the stranger on the other end of the line.

"Hello?" The caller seemed puzzled by her silence.

"I'm still here, Mr. Parker," Sarah said weakly. "It's just...well, I haven't had an opportunity to discuss this with Farrell."

"Discuss what, Mom?" Somehow, Mike had managed to reclaim his soccer ball. Now, with the cocky grin of a boy getting away with something, he bounced it across the room and down the hall. The man was speaking again, but because of the noise, Sarah missed what he said. "Mike," she yelled, "put that ball down this minute and finish your dinner."

"You have two sons, Mrs. Michaels?"

"Lord, no," Sarah said, not knowing why she found the question humorous—unless it was because she didn't seem to be dealing well with even *one* son tonight. "His name is Farrell. He prefers to be called Mike."

"I see. Mrs. Michaels, since your son's right there, do you suppose you could discuss it with him and decide? I live across town. This would be a good time for us to get together, lay down some ground rules."

Ground rules. Sarah liked the sound of that and she liked his voice. "Forgive me, Mr. Parker," she said, making the decision on the spur of the moment. "I realize you've volunteered precious free time. Come on over and I'll fill him in before you get here. Do you need our address?"

"No, ma'am. It's on my introduction papers. It'll take me about fifteen minutes. Will that give you enough time?"

"That'll be fine," she murmured, smoothing a hand down her stew-spattered blouse. He made her feel old, calling her ma'am, and she wanted to change into something clean. But Mr. Parker wasn't coming to see her. Besides, he was probably used to dealing with disheveled mothers. Mr. Evans from the agency said he'd had his last assignment three years, she recalled.

The caller clicked off and Sarah was left holding a buzzing phone. Thrown in a sudden panic, she hurried to the kitchen and shouted for Mike.

He appeared in the doorway, looking nervous. "Don't take my soccer ball away, Mom. I won't bounce it in the house again. Honest!"

Sarah cleared her throat, stacked the bills, then asked abruptly, "Do any of your friends at school have men they spend time with who aren't their fathers?"

"Sure, Mom. Danny Ruggles has an uncle who picks him up. Some of the guys do things with their mom's boyfriends." He sat down. "'Course, they aren't stuffy like yours."

Sarah's breath escaped in a slow hiss. "If you mean Harvey Denton, he is *not* my boyfriend. He's an associate in the law firm where I work. Occasionally he invites me to go with him to a performance or community function." She caught herself sounding priggish and dropped into the chair beside her son. "Anyway, I didn't mean boyfriends. Ah, have you ever heard of a program called Befriend an Island Child?"

He shook his head.

"Well, sometimes people volunteer to spend time with children who have only one parent. To be a grown-up friend to them. Men for fatherless boys and women for motherless girls. A friend wouldn't have as much time as a real father, you understand," she rushed to say when his eyes sparked with interest. "Some volunteers have families of their own. At the most, a man might have a few hours a month to spend."

"You mean someone might have spare time to kick a soccer ball around with a kid?" He brushed biscuit crumbs into a neat pile, looking hopeful.

"Yes, or at least, I assume so." Now Sarah was worried. Not all men were sports enthusiasts. Take Harvey, for instance. She should have thought to ask Gabe Parker that all-important question.

"Do you think I could get a friend, Mom? Will you call them guys tomorrow? I'd like one by this weekend." He ran the whole mouthful of words together without taking a breath.

"Whoa," she said. "It's *those* guys, and there's no guarantee, Mike. The decision is up to the volunteer." Then, because he looked so crestfallen, she quickly explained about Gabe Parker.

"Wow, that's neat! Can I call him Gabe or will I have to call him Mr. Parker?"

Sarah wanted to stay calm, but it was hard not to catch fire from his enthusiasm. "We'll have to ask him. Remember, some volunteers are older."

"But he won't be boring like Harvey, will he?"

Sarah closed her eyes. It was clear she needed to talk with Mike about Harvey Denton, but right now, Harvey wasn't the issue. Reaching out, she smoothed her son's hair and smiled. For Mike's sake she hoped Mr. Parker liked soccer, but it would be nice if he also enjoyed museums, fine art and good music. Mike would benefit from that, too.

"You in a better mood now, Mom?" Astute blue eyes searched her face.

Sarah touched a finger to his nose. "Was I so bad earlier? Is there something special on your mind?"

"Maybe I should wait... for my new friend." The small boy's eyes rounded anxiously. "Coach said we oughtta ask our parents tonight about soccer camp. It's at the university this summer. We'd get to stay for a whole week. Lotsa pro players come to teach kids like us. Almost all my team is goin'." His eyes changed, suddenly alight with excitement.

"Oh, no, Mike." First Sarah needed to correct his misconception. "These *friends* don't pay for things like camp." She bit her lip. "Just how expensive are we talking, anyway?"

The sparkle died and his freckles stood out against his pinched white face.

Sarah's heart took a nosedive. It wasn't right to involve him in her financial woes. He was just a child. "Well, how much?" she prompted, trying to sound optimistic.

"A hundred and seventy-five dollars," he mumbled. "But that 'cludes food and a place to sleep. Coach said."

Sarah gasped. "That's more than I need to fix the air conditioner."

"Don't care!" He leapt out of his chair and snatched up his soccer ball. "All the guys are goin'. It's 'portant." With that, he slammed out the back door, uncaring that his chair fell over and hit the floor or that the front doorbell had just chimed.

Nerves stretched to the limit, Sarah righted the chair. On her way down the hall, she said a prayer that Mr. Gabe Parker had the patience to deal with unhappy little boys and frazzled mothers. Then, because the bell pealed three times in succession, she decided he didn't. Girding herself to meet some rushed executive, Sarah yanked open the door, then stood gaping in stunned silence.

It was worse than she could have imagined. A broad-shouldered, suntanned hunk in raggedy cutoffs was shrugging into a faded Hawaiian-print shirt as he loped back down her front steps. And beside her dented silver Mustang sat a shiny blue Porsche, draped stem to stern with a banana-yellow surfboard.

This was all some terrible mistake, Sarah thought frantically. It wasn't the man from the agency. It was just a tourist who had strayed off the beach road and needed directions. She felt better already. "May I help you?" she called.

The stranger turned and squinted up at her. "Is this the Michaels residence?" he asked pleasantly. It was the same deep voice Sarah had heard on the phone. Having buttoned his shirt halfway up from the bottom, he left it. She stared at a wide expanse of sun-bronzed chest with a swirl of pale gold hair. *No!* she wanted to scream. She wanted to slam her door, pull the drapes and hide. So strong was the feeling she almost missed the apology he was offering.

"Gabriel Parker. Gabe. Sorry about the casual clothes," he said around a very unsorry grin. Or at least that was how it looked to Sarah.

He tipped his head to one side and gave a comical shrug. "I have to confess. It was so hot today I played hooky from work this afternoon and went to the beach. But I'm sure you understand." The man spread his palms and narrowed his gaze, obviously not sure she did.

Speech lodged in Sarah's throat. She was blinded by an aura that ringed his head. Kind of an off-kilter halo created by the last rays of sun splintering through his too-long, wind-mussed, taffy-blond hair. Hysteria rose and suddenly her nagging headache turned into a full-scale migraine.

"Are *you* Mrs. Michaels?" he asked. "Forgive me for saying so, but you look too young to be anyone's mother, and this neighborhood is a cut above what I was expecting." He glanced around.

His smooth compliment snapped Sarah out of her reverie as nothing else could. Although he was taller and not so slender as Farrell, this man's attire, his practiced charm and his shiny surf board might have been cloned. No way would she let this younger version of her ex-husband near her son!

Sarah glared down at him. "I never claimed to be destitute. I'm looking for a stabilizing influence for my son, Mr. Parker. Not some...some irresponsible surf bum. I'm sorry you've come out of your way, but this arrangement is not at all acceptable."

"I beg your pardon?" He moved up a step and met her eye to eye.

"Beg all you want." Her lips tightened.

He pulled a wrinkled letter out of his back pocket and gave it to her. "A recommendation from Bill Evans may ease your mind. It says I've lived on Oahu all my life and that I own a business in Waikiki."

The note also mentioned the Parker hotels that were his background, but Gabe tended to play that down. And this woman didn't seem to care if he was King Midas himself. She gave no sign of reading the letter. Out of frustration, Gabe retaliated. "Bill Evans told me you were pretty uptight, but he didn't say..."

Sarah's hands clenched. *"Uptight?"* she interrupted. "You know nothing at all about me, Mr. Parker. I'd like you to go. Please...just leave." She thrust back his letter. "Believe me, this won't work."

"You bet. I couldn't agree more." He stuffed the envelope into the tight pocket of his shorts. Backing down a step, he asked stiffly, "Will you call the agency or shall I?"

Before Sarah could snap that there was plenty she had to say to Mr. Evans, the family coordinator and director at Befriend an Island Child, a blue-and-white soccer ball sailed over the side fence, hit a crack in the sidewalk and careered wildly toward her head.

Quick as a cat, Gabe Parker reached out a broad hand and stopped it from striking her in the face.

Somewhere close by, a gate slammed. All at once the sturdy figure of her son loped into sight.

"Farr...Mike...oh, no," Sarah cried faintly. "No. Stay back."

Seeing the adults on the steps, the boy skidded to a stop and hung his tousled head. "Sorry," he said, obviously in awe of the tall golden-haired stranger. "I don't kick so good. Coach said."

Sarah closed her eyes and slumped against the door. "Why me, Lord?" she muttered.

Gabe Parker sent her a dark look and dropped to one knee. He closed the child's trembling hands around the ball and said gently, "Try using the side of your foot next time, instead of your toe. You'll control the ball better."

"Wow!" The freckled little face lit up. "Will you show me how?"

Parker frowned. His cool gaze clashed with Sarah's. Then he stood and massaged the back of his neck. "I was just leaving."

Gabe didn't have a clue as to what was going on inside her head, but it was plain she didn't like him. And frankly the feeling was mutual.

The child darted a furtive glance toward his mother, then back to Gabe. "I don't guess you wanna be my friend, after all, huh, Mr. Parker? Mom said you might not..."

Sarah stifled a cry of protest as Gabe turned the full force of ice-blue eyes her way. Damn him! Couldn't he see she was trapped? After all, he had agreed it wouldn't work. But it was to her the boy looked with his heart in his eyes. She shut hers and vigorously rubbed her temples. Maybe she'd wake up and find this was all just a ghastly dream. But she opened her eyes and felt overwhelmed to find nothing had changed.

Gabe saw the panic in her sherry-brown eyes, but he also saw something more. He saw how much she loved this boy. That alone prompted him to give his mission another try. Although, for the life of him, Gabe couldn't imagine why, when the agency had a lot less-difficult people on the waiting list. Placing a foot on the lowest step, he faced her, gaze steady. "What do you say we both give this some thought tonight and discuss it again tomorrow?"

His voice rumbled in Sarah's head. She nodded mutely. Right now, more than anything in the world, she wanted him gone.

CHAPTER TWO

ALL IN ALL, Gabe Parker had been more decent than Sarah expected. After agreeing that she should call Mr. Evans the next day to ask about a replacement, he still offered to drop by around four to help Mike with his kicking. They could discuss the outcome then, he said.

Ecstatic, Mike took his bath and went to bed without argument.

Sarah had to admit she should have been less grudging with her thanks, particularly since Parker had helped her out of a tight spot. Of course, they both knew how it would end. Even so, he could have walked away and left her to deal with disappointment and tears. But, unless Mr. Evans at the agency could produce a miracle, she had one day's reprieve at best.

Laundry done but not sorted, Sarah showered and fell exhausted into bed. She tossed and turned all night and finally managed to doze off toward morning.

At 6 a.m. she was pulled from her sleep by a loud crash. Disoriented, sleepy-eyed, she squinted up at the shadowy outline of her son. Closer inspection showed him looking guilty, clutching a plastic tray on which a stack of charred toast lay awash in water from a slender vase. And could that be a delicate baby orchid floating in a muddy cup of coffee? "Is this Mother's Day?" Sarah croaked. "I know it's not my birthday."

"I'm real sorry, Mom," the shaken child said. "I was just bringin' you breakfast in bed—'cause I acted so crummy last night."

Her son's repentant look cut through to Sarah's heart and drove away all lingering vestiges of sleep. She smiled. "How nice. I must be the luckiest mother on Oahu. Orchids with breakfast—like in the best hotels."

The boy's chest puffed in pride. The precarious dishes rattled.

Sarah sat up and shrugged into her robe. Then she accepted the tray. Plucking the flower from the cup, she sniffed the coffee-drenched blossom.

"Since this is a workday for me and a schoolday for you," she said diplomatically, "why don't we go to the kitchen where we can eat together? I'll carry the tray."

He waited while she climbed out of bed, then preceded her down the hall. "I'm real sorry 'bout the accident with the vase, Mom. Sorry 'bout last night too. Aunt Mitzi told me before how hard you work to pay bills." Wriggling into the breakfast nook, he promptly hefted a spoonful of soggy cereal he'd left waiting. "I jus' wanna do some things the guys who have dads do. Like fishin'."

Fishing? Sarah took her seat. That was news to her.

He kicked his feet against the table leg. "I know fishin' costs money. But now I got Gabe. It's gonna be better, ain't it, Mom?"

"*Ain't,* Mike?" Sarah took a big gulp of cold coffee, forgetting it had been laced with orchid nectar. After choking and partially recovering, she lectured, "Mike, Mr. Parker isn't... He..." She gave up and waved a hand. The boy looked stubborn as he slurped milk from his bowl.

"Farrell! Stop that this minute. It's rude. And I thought we covered this yesterday. No matter who ends up being your friend, you don't ever ask him to buy you *anything.* I want your promise."

"But I thought..." Red splotches stained his cheeks. "'Sides, you promised to call me Mike. And do I gotta call him Mr. Parker tonight?"

Sarah scraped furiously at the burned toast. "I, uh... Oh, look, it's time for you to get ready for school." She set the toast aside. "You take the school bus home today. Call

Mitzi's mom if he doesn't show up, okay? I'll be home right after work."

Lower lip quivering, Mike pushed his dish aside and ran from the room.

Coward, she berated herself. Why didn't she just tell him Gabe Parker was probably no more dependable than his father had been? *Because,* she answered herself, *he's only a boy and he doesn't deserve more heartache.*

Back in her room, Sarah soon discovered it would take more than makeup to hide the ravages of a sleepless night.

As they were leaving the house, Mike hugged his soccer ball and said staunchly, "Gabe'll show up. I know." He barely stood still for Sarah to give his unruly cowlick a last swipe with a comb.

For an unguarded moment, she, too, was affected by the hope shimmering in his eyes. Yet what could she do? What could she say?

Sarah had dropped Mike off at school and was nearing Mitzi's place when the magnitude of the mess she was in really hit her. Mitzi had no more than put one foot in the car when Sarah spilled her entire story.

"Wow!" her friend exclaimed. "Quite a night. Frankly, I can't see your problem."

"I said he *skipped* work to go surfing."

"My brothers surf every chance they get. Sam, too. Not all surfers are flakes, you know. Maybe he had time off, or something."

Sarah didn't look convinced.

Mitzi rolled her eyes. "You're not planning to marry the guy, are you?"

"Certainly not." Sarah was indignant.

"Well, then, go with the flow."

"Mitzi, I swear, haven't you heard a thing I said? He wore thongs and disreputable cutoffs. Would you want a man like that influencing your son?"

"This is Hawaii. And you said he apologized for the way he looked."

Sarah stopped her car in front of the import firm where Mitzi worked. "I know," she said reluctantly, "but Farrell did, too, when it suited him."

Mitzi placed a calming hand on Sarah's arm. "You can't judge every man you meet by Farrell Michaels."

Sarah gazed out at the array of boats anchored in the bay. She made no comment.

Sighing, Mitzi slid from the car.

"'Bye," Sarah said without enthusiasm. "See you at five."

"Later, gator," Mitzi chirped. Grinning, she leaned down and flashed Sarah the rocking thumb-little finger hang-loose sign of the islands.

That at least made Sarah smile. But her problems closed in again before she reached her own workplace.

In the elevator, it occurred to her that her boss, Lou Page, might offer some sound advice.

Encouraged, she entered her office, shoved her purse into a lower desk drawer and readied her computer for the day. Then she tapped quietly on Lou's door.

"Come in," his deep voice boomed.

She peeked in. "Good morning. Do you have a minute?"

The big man swiveled his chair away from the window with its full ocean view. "Always for you, Sarah. Gad, you look terrible today. Are you sick? Or is it Junior?"

Lou never called her son Farrell, and she hadn't told him about the nickname. "Thanks a lot! Edna should teach you better manners," she teased.

He reddened slightly. "Forgive me. I didn't mean—"

"It's okay." Sarah sat across from him. She knew that Edna, Lou's wife of forty years, worked diligently to hone his rough edges. "No one's sick, Lou. I'd like to ask you about the Befriend an Island Child program. Remember I said I'd signed up?"

"I remember. If I recall, both Harvey and I thought it was a good idea." Glancing over her shoulder, the older man waved someone in.

Sarah turned. Harvey Denton—one of the junior law partners, a dapper man in his late thirties—stood at the door, looking puzzled.

"Isn't that right, Harvey?" Lou confirmed.

The newcomer fingered his arrow-straight tie. "I thought I heard my name. What's the topic under discussion today?"

Sarah chewed her lip. She hadn't wanted to involve Harvey. "I came to ask Lou's opinion of a man by the name of Gabriel Parker," she said, deciding it was too late now. "Befriend an Island Child assigned my son to him."

Lou whistled, and Harvey frowned.

"What?" Sarah burst out. "Do you two know something?"

Harvey helped himself to a chair. After adjusting the creases in his pants, he said, "It's hard to believe a man of Parker's stature would volunteer to schlepp around with kids."

"Children *are* people, Harvey," Sarah said hotly.

"Gabriel Parker is heir to a monolithic conglomerate. I can't get a foot in the door of the Parkers' infrastructure, although they know perfectly well we could serve them better than Gibson, Gibson and Frane."

"This isn't about business, Harvey," Sarah pointed out. But his comments did explain Parker's attitude toward work. "Is he a fit companion for a child? That's what I need to know."

Lou tilted back in his chair. "The agency has a sterling reputation."

Harvey patted Sarah's hand. "I, for one, would be happy to see you manage a few free evenings."

Sarah felt her cheeks heat under Harvey's personal comments. "I'm not doubting the program's value." She turned back to Lou. "Yesterday, when he came by to introduce himself, Parker looked like some beach bum."

Lou laughed. "Grandpa Parker built boats. Old renegade surfed till he died. Didn't you request someone sports-minded for Junior?"

"Well, yes." Now she floundered. "Uh, Lou, don't call him Junior anymore. He wants people to call him Mike. I promised I would."

"Great idea," Lou agreed. "It's hardly any secret how I feel about Senior. I've always blamed myself that you met the devil in my office."

Sarah stood. "I'd better get to work and quit wasting time. Thanks, anyway. I believe I'll see if the agency has anyone else available."

The older man looked thoughtful. "I'll do some discreet checking today if you'd like."

"Would you?" She smiled gratefully. "I'd like to know. Maybe the agency doesn't screen as well as they should."

Harvey followed her out, polishing a gold cuff link on his sleeve. "I've got tickets to the opera Friday. Care to go?"

Sarah brightened, then looked away and frowned. "I can't Friday. Mitzi and I are going to Mike's soccer game, then out for pizza afterward."

"Soccer and pizza," he sneered. "How could *La Bohème* ever compete with that? Ask Mitzi to baby-sit."

"La Bohème?" she repeated wistfully, then shook her head. "This is kind of a trial game against another island team, Harvey. It's important that I go."

"Suit yourself." He smoothed his expertly groomed hair. "I won't have trouble finding another date."

A terse retort rose to Sarah's tongue, but she held it in check. She certainly didn't have any claim on Harvey's life, nor he on hers. "Maybe next time," she offered, picking up a stack of files from her desk.

"Maybe," he growled. "Maybe you can work out something with Parker. Macho types wallow in physical competition—like soccer. Just take care you don't let the boy become another dumb jock, though."

"Thank you, Mr. Denton," Sarah said dryly. "I'll take that under advisement." Had Harvey always been bossy, or was she just more tired than normal? Tired probably, Sarah thought, sliding a tape into her dictaphone.

Off and on all day she tried reaching Mr. Evans at the agency. When at last she did get through, he seemed totally taken aback by her call.

"Mrs. Michaels," he said sharply, after she'd questioned Gabe Parker's credentials, "Gabriel is one of our most prominent volunteers. I think you should know we have more children than friends—there's no one else available. If you have doubts, perhaps this isn't the program for you. I'll place him with the next child on the list."

No one else available. Suddenly Sarah envisioned Mike's disappointment. She recalled the spark in his eyes this morning. "No, wait," she implored. "I, ah..." Although she felt strongly that she'd never have any rapport with Parker herself, when push came to shove Sarah couldn't deny her son. "He's dropping by my house again this afternoon. Would you give me until tomorrow to decide?"

"Fine," the agency coordinator agreed. "But not one day longer."

Sarah felt pressured as she hung up and resumed her typing. She should have just declined. It wasn't going to work.

She was leaving for the day when Lou stopped her. "Sarah, do you have a minute? I made several calls today. You'll be interested to know the hotel people gave Parker the best of references."

"Could you be more specific, please, Lou? I'm not looking to build a hotel. I'm concerned about his character."

Lou smiled. "Wish you'd been this cautious when you met Farrell."

Sarah groaned. "Not fair, Lou. Besides, two wrongs don't make a right. And Mike's too young to distinguish hero worship from what's real."

Lou shrugged. "Only thing anyone said on the minus side was that young Parker frequently makes the society news—always with a different woman."

"Wonderful! What'd I tell you? Another playboy surfer."

"You really believe he's a jerk, don't you, Sarah? As a rule, beach boys aren't featured on the society page."

"I wouldn't know." Sarah frowned. "I stopped taking the paper. I'm too tired to read it, anyway. And it's an expense we don't need."

"Time for a raise?"

Sarah flushed. "I wasn't hinting, Lou. You're quite generous."

"Apparently not if you can't afford the damn paper. I'll talk with the others tomorrow. Surely fifty dollars a month is in order."

Sarah hugged him impulsively. "Even ten dollars would come in handy now that I have to replace my car's air conditioner."

"Is it time I go hunting Farrell again? Why don't you tell me when he quits sending support?"

Sarah averted her gaze. "Because you're busy enough. Because I can't pay you for the legwork and, if you must know, I don't like the hard-luck stories he has DeeDee write me when he does finally send a few dollars."

Lou snorted. "It's news to me that woman can write. Dammit, Sarah. The man cleaned out your bank account. He took what your dad left you for upkeep on the house."

Sarah moved toward the door. She didn't dare tell Lou that Farrell thought he'd *earned* the money—suffering through a marriage with someone he called "an albatross." Once he found out she was pregnant, he considered the money he took his due for "services rendered." He'd said as much in a room filled with his surfing crowd one day. Even now, the memory humiliated her.

"I have to pick up Mitzi," she said abruptly. "Thanks again for all you've done. See you tomorrow, Lou."

"You're the daughter I never had, Sarah," the old attorney muttered. "If I ever see Farrell again, I might just strangle him with my bare hands."

Times like these, Sarah thought she might just let him.

Mitzi waited on the corner in the humid heat. "Where've you been?" she said when Sarah pulled up. "I bought us soft drinks, but they're warming up."

"Sorry I'm late." Sarah accepted her cup gratefully. "I was talking with Lou and the time got away."

"Oh?" A delicate black brow shot up. "Did you, by any chance, ask him to shake Farrell's tree again?"

"I didn't ask. He volunteered. Actually, I asked him to run a check on Gabe Parker. The conversation digressed from there."

"Really?" Mitzi shook back her long black hair and took a swallow of soda. "I polled my office today. All women." She grinned. "I doubt you want to hear about all the panting. I must say I can't wait to vet this hunk. Word is, he has money *and* great pecs."

"Exactly," Sarah sniffed. "I'm sure he's the god of Muscle Beach. But I don't happen to feel like falling on my knees when he flexes his biceps." She made a face. "What'll I do?" she wailed. "Mike will hate me if I nix Parker. But what'll he learn from a guy like that?"

"Well, he'd have all the third-grade girls at his feet."

"Mitzi."

"Okay, okay. I was joking." Mitzi held the cool cup to her cheek. "Way I see it, you don't have much choice. Give it a whirl. If he turns out to be a skunk, I'll have Osamu break him in half."

Sarah laughed. "Mitzi, my friend, without you I'd never laugh." She swung into the Kealohas' drive. "Now scram. I don't want to be late. If Parker shows up and I'm not there, he'll think I'm a lousy mother."

"Call me, huh? Let me know what you decide. Suspense kills me."

"I wish I'd made arrangements for Mike to stay at your mom's after school. It'll be harder to be objective with him there." Suddenly she snagged Mitzi's arm. "Do you think I'm wishy-washy?"

Mitzi paused, half in, half out of the car. "I think you're trying to be two people. Supermom and Superdad rolled into one. But that's positively all I'm going to say on the subject. G'night."

Heading home, Sarah took side streets, hoping to beat the traffic.

Bang!

Sarah jumped as though she'd been shot. Her car began to wobble. "Wouldn't you know it?" she seethed. "Not a tourist to be seen and me with a blown tire." Well, she'd changed tires before. It didn't mean she liked tackling one in this heat. And no telephone, either—not that she had anyone to call. She climbed out to survey the situation.

At least her spare tire had air in it. Which wasn't always the case. Sarah muscled it out of the trunk and wrinkled her nose at the grease that came out of nowhere to stain her khaki skirt. But grease was only the beginning. Before long, sweat molded her blouse to her back and she had grit under her fingernails—those she hadn't snapped off. Her hair tumbled from its clasp and clung wetly to her neck long before she had the tire mounted. Frazzled, she wiped her hands on an old towel she found in the trunk and slammed the lid closed.

When she finally arrived home and saw the blue Porsche, she groaned. To make matters worse, the blasted thing looked as if it had been newly waxed and polished for the occasion. She crawled out of her tired old Mustang and shut the door viciously. Her high heels clacked against the concrete walkway as she approached the house. When she tried the front door and found it locked, she gnashed her teeth. Darn. Where the heck were they?

Then she heard noises in her backyard. A boyish laugh, followed by a man's deeper tones. Her heart skipped a beat. She hadn't realized until now how often she'd dreamed of hearing such sounds.

Quietly she tiptoed over to the side gate. The sinking sun shot threads of gold through two bright caps of hair. Even from this distance, Sarah could see her son's eyes gazing intently up into Parker's—which were the same deep blue as his own.

A bell sounded a warning in her head. *Those two could pass for father and son.* Sarah felt an unreasonable urge to race in there and snatch her child away. "That's silly," she whispered. But in her distress, she dropped her purse.

The noise attracted the man's attention. He tossed Mike the soccer ball and rushed over to retrieve her scattered things. "What happened?" he asked, looking up at Sarah's smudged face. "Are you all right? You weren't in an accident?"

Sarah didn't like him at her feet, didn't like the fact that he was so clean in his white pants and crisp shirt. Especially compared to her... Movements stiff, she stepped backward. "I had a flat tire, that's all," she said as her son came bounding over. "Sorry I'm late."

"Wow, Mom, I didn't even know you was late. Gabe and me are havin' fun."

"Gabe and *I* are having fun," Sarah corrected automatically. "And it's *were* late."

The boy cocked his head. "But you wasn't here."

"Mike," she said in exasperation. Then realizing her voice had risen, she sighed and blotted a cheek with her forearm. "Did you ask if you could call him Gabe?" She snatched her purse out of Parker's hands and felt a small shock as their fingers touched.

"He did," the man said, slow to draw back his hand. "I hope you don't mind. If he called me Mr. Parker, I'd be looking around for my dad."

Sarah sighed again.

Gabe studied her a moment and saw the tiredness. "You look like you've had a rough day. We could postpone this meeting."

"No," Sarah almost snapped. "Mr. Evans wants my decision tomorrow. We may as well get it over with."

"You make it sound like an execution," he said half under his breath. More loudly he continued, "Why don't you relax a few minutes, Mrs. Michaels? I'm sure you'd like to shower and change. Mike and I'll finish practice."

Sarah didn't want him being so damned magnanimous when she was acting like a shrew. She didn't want him here, period. Yet she could see from the adoration on Mike's face her problems were multiplying like rabbits.

"Thanks," she said grudgingly. "I won't be long."

"Take your time, Mom," Mike yelled. "Gabe's teachin' me how to kick."

"Great...wonderful," she muttered, trudging through the back door, ruing the day soccer was invented.

Surprisingly Sarah did feel refreshed by a shower. As she dressed in navy cotton pants and a white oversize shirt, she speculated that a suit might give her more of an advantage when it came to negotiations with Parker. Oh, well...

Leaving the comfort of her room, she headed for the kitchen, expecting to find them still playing soccer in the yard. But as she pushed open the French doors, she stopped short. Both of them stood at her kitchen counter calmly shaping hamburger meat into patties. Mike was yammering nonstop. He paused for a breath only after his tall companion nudged him. "Hi, Mom." The boy grinned. "Me and Gabe are fixin' dinner." A wayward lock of hair fell across his eye, and he blew it away before plunging his hands into the sticky meat mixture again.

"Gabe and I," Sarah said without thinking.

"Are you gonna help, too?" The child's blue eyes grew wider still. "We're doin' this 'cause Gabe thinks you look beat—like the last rose of...of...something." He glanced to the man for help.

"Ah, 'summer' was what I said, Mike." Gabe met her narrowed gaze with a sheepish grin. "I see now that 'the last rose of summer' was the wrong expression, Mrs. Michaels. Or may I call you Sarah?" he asked, taking a second inventory.

Oblivious to the undercurrent swirling between the two adults, the child hummed to himself as he carefully placed a patty on a sheet of waxed paper.

Sarah turned abruptly toward her son. "I was correcting your bad English, Mike," she explained. "Please try to use better grammar." Irritated by Parker's earlier statement about her appearance, she said, "Not everyone can spend a leisurely afternoon bumming around the beach. Some of us work for a living."

Gabe knew the barb was aimed at him. He refused to acknowledge her ill humor. Instead, he turned away to wash his hands.

It was then that Sarah saw the table was set for three. That, too, irked her.

"Did you invite Mr. Parker to dinner without asking, Mike? You know the house rules."

Her son's happy grin faded.

Feeling like a heel, Sarah wished she'd just let the incident slide. After all, it was late, and she had to settle this issue with Parker tonight.

"I thought it was only friends my age I hadda ask about," the boy said. "Gabe's different, isn't he, Mom?"

As if he wasn't the one under discussion, Gabe calmly set a salad bowl filled with greens in the refrigerator. Trying to remain unobtrusive, he leaned against the counter and waited. He sensed her mood was erratic.

Sarah had to appreciate the fact that he didn't try to interfere. Backing off, she threw up her hands and gave a weak smile. "Forget I said anything, guys. I *am* beat tonight. I should be gracious and thank you both for fixing dinner." She glanced hesitantly at their guest as she ran a nervous hand through her son's curls.

She was rewarded by the return of Gabe's heart-stopping smile.

"You're a good mother, Mrs. Michaels," he said in an undertone when the conversation lagged. "This is all my fault. You'd gone to shower when I noticed the barbecue out back. Mike mentioned the meat was thawed—"

Sarah interrupted with something unintelligible. Then, as if by prior agreement, all three of them moved to the backyard where Gabe set about preparing the ancient barbecue. Sarah watched, aware of how easily he dispatched chores that took her much longer. And Mike, who ordinarily wouldn't have a thing to do with cooking, begged to help.

Sarah found that funny. But her smile died as her gaze accidentally collided with Gabe's. She blushed. *Certainly he didn't read anything untoward into my laughter, did he?*

Sobering, she decided to set the record straight. With Mike in the house to hunt up barbecue sauce, she approached Gabe. She had to let him know she wasn't his type—in case he was considering it, which she doubted—and she wasn't looking for a husband substitute or any fake family togetherness. She took a deep breath. "I'm not much good at impromptu picnics, Mr. Parker. Or impromptu anything. You may as well hear this up front. My inability to do these... these spur-of-the-moment things is a major reason Mike's father left us." She let her lashes drop to hide her embarrassment. It sounded awful spelled out. What must he think?

Bold blue eyes inspected her from the crown of her head to her trim ankles, then moved slowly back up again. "Some men are natural fools," Gabe said, his voice matter-of-fact.

Sarah wasn't sure she'd heard correctly. Nevertheless her cheeks burned, and she was relieved when Mike returned to claim Parker's attention. She went back inside where she rearranged the table settings, placing them far enough apart to avoid any suggestion of intimacy. When there was nothing left to do, she stepped out on the back deck to see when dinner would be ready.

The charcoal briquettes chose that moment to erupt in flames. It all happened so fast Sarah's feet stayed rooted to the planks. She watched in horror as smoke billowed and flames reached treacherous fingers toward her son. A cry welled up but lodged in her throat.

Gabe, appearing calm, set the child behind him and fanned through the smoke to lift the sizzling rack away from the flames. "Could you get me a cup of water, please, Mike?" he asked quietly. "You see now why I said we should never stand close to the barrel when we light it."

Big-eyed, Mike nodded, then turned and ran past his mother to fetch water from the kitchen. He jostled her on the way out. "Move, Mom! Gabe needs this quick."

Sarah's heart began a slow slide back into place. Her knees buckled. She sank onto the top step and stared. Gabe sprinkled water over the hot coals, all the while explaining to Mike what he was doing and why. Once the steam had dissipated, he let his little helper place the first patty on the grill.

Sarah heard the praise mixed with his instructions. She wished she could honestly say she would have handled things this well. But she knew from past experience that she probably would have panicked, frantically dashed water at the flames, yelled at Mike to get out of the way. He'd have burst into tears, and if they ate at all the meal would have been tense.

She rose and stumbled toward the house. Part of her had wanted Gabe Parker to fall short in his dealings with her son. But what if he had? He spoke at her elbow, making her jump.

"Charbroiled hamburger, madam?" He whisked a plate over her shoulder and with a grandiose flourish leaned around her and waggled his eyebrows.

She eyed the blackened patty. "Charred would be more accurate," she said, wrinkling her nose. As she ducked beneath his arm, she caught the anxious look on her son's face. "However—" she backpedaled "—I'm hungry enough to eat mine raw." The boy's relieved grin would have been redeeming if Gabe's presence hadn't made her so edgy.

She suddenly realized there were no glasses on the table. "I don't keep beer in the house," she said to Gabe. "Would you like water or milk?"

"There's lemonade. Mike picked lemons from your tree and made it all by himself." Gabe indicated the frosty pitcher.

Sarah's surprise showed. "Well, by all means, we must have lemonade." Pleased, she gave Mike a spontaneous hug.

He grinned but eluded her to follow Gabe's lead in slapping condiments on his hamburger bun.

Sarah set the pitcher of lemonade and three glasses on the table. Her son emulated Gabe's every move—down to the dill-pickle garnish he ordinarily loathed. Quickly she bit into her own hamburger, unwilling to admit she might be just a bit jealous.

Sarah had intended to remain coolly aloof. Before she knew it, however, she was laughing along with Mike at Gabe's sports stories—none of which included surfing. It was after one such humorous anecdote that she happened to glance at her watch.

"Mike," she gasped, "it's almost nine! Tomorrow's a school day. Bedtime."

She dismissed his "Aw, Mom" and his pout with a firm shake of her head. Now, she thought, comes the tantrum. Parker would see firsthand what she had to deal with.

Unfolding his rangy length from the table, Gabe commanded, "Do as your mother says, Mike. Ordinarily I'd expect you to help clean up, but tonight we adults have things to discuss, so you're off the hook."

Mike jumped up. "Okay, but will you come say g'night 'fore you go?"

"If I can." Their guest darted a sharp glance in Sarah's direction.

Dumbfounded at the way he'd backed her, Sarah nodded.

Mike bestowed one last puppy-dog grin on Gabe, then left the room.

Suddenly the kitchen seemed too small and too quiet to suit Sarah. "I'll make coffee," she offered, leaping to her feet.

"I'd like that," Gabe said as he tried to discreetly dump an almost full glass of lemonade down the drain.

She laughed and suddenly the constraints fell away. "I saw that. I should make you drink the rest of that horrible stuff. Why didn't you tell him to add sugar?"

Gabe chuckled and turned from loading the dishwasher. "I couldn't believe you drank yours with a straight face. You deserve a medal. It's just... he was so proud. I didn't have the heart to burst his bubble."

Sarah swallowed a giant lump. "Take a seat, Mr. Parker. So far, you've done all the work. The least I can do is dishes." She placed milk, sugar and mugs on the table, and her smile flashed again.

"Call me Gabe, please. May I say…it was good to see you relax." He smiled back and slid into the nook. "I know I made a bad first impression. What can I do or say to change your opinion, Sarah?" Her first name slipped easily off his tongue, because somehow she was different tonight. Gabe thought perhaps this might work out, after all.

A chill of apprehension skated up Sarah's spine. Mesmerized by the brilliant blue eyes so like her son's, she found her thoughts muddled. Losing count of how many teaspoons of instant coffee she'd put into each cup, she gave up and poured the boiling water. Catching her lip between her teeth, she turned the handle of one toward him. "You certainly won Mike over fast." She drew back quickly as their fingers accidentally brushed. Again a shock.

"I like him," Gabe stated simply. "I like most kids, but he seems exceptionally bright." He gazed beyond her into the distance. "My father was always too busy building an empire to spend time with my brother and me. Perhaps I relate to Mike's loneliness."

Sarah hid her surprise. It was difficult to believe he was ever lonely. He possessed the type of unconscious good looks women fawned over. Farrell did, too—and he'd had the same effect on women. She gulped her coffee, glad of the heat that burned her mouth and took her mind off her feelings about Gabe Parker.

The moment the sting subsided, she broached the subject she'd mulled over all day. "The agency has no other volunteer available and my son needs help with soccer. So if you're still interested, it's okay by me. Any time you could spare to teach him will be appreciated. But I'd like to approve all arrangements in advance. And if you aren't able to follow through, I'll expect time to break the news. He's been disappointed quite enough already." Gabe sipped from his cup and studied her without blinking.

For several moments Sarah thought he would refuse.

At last he shrugged. "He's your son. You set the rules. I follow them. Our program isn't designed to antagonize parents." Gabe put down his cup. The tension was back between them.

Sarah broke eye contact first. Before she had a chance to respond, Mike stuck his fresh-scrubbed face around the corner. "Will you tuck me in, Gabe?" His expression was anxious, as if he expected things to have changed since he'd left.

"If it's okay with your mom, kicker." Gabe slid out of his chair.

Sarah was too tired to fight them both. "Don't be surprised if you can't find his bed for the stuffed animals," she told Gabe. Picking up their cups, she walked to the sink. "It's late, so please make it quick. I'll be in the living room."

She had just begun to wonder what was keeping Gabe, when he reappeared, looking slightly abashed.

"He conned me into reading a story."

Abruptly Sarah said, "Please don't give him so much attention that he'll be hurt when you finish this assignment, Mr. Parker." Her warning loomed between them like a gathering summer storm.

"I thought we'd progressed to Gabe and Sarah. And he's not *just* an assignment. If you could drop the chip off your shoulder a minute, I'd like a word with you about those soccer shoes of his."

"What about them?" she asked, rising. "Coach gave them to him. They were his son's."

"Ah. That explains it." Gabe was relieved to hear she hadn't bought them. "They're too small," he said. "He needs a new pair before Friday."

"Mike hasn't said they hurt his feet," Sarah said defensively. "It's not like he wears them all the time. I hope you didn't fill his head with foolishness. I have a mortgage to pay, bills, a car air conditioner to replace—" She broke off. Her finances did not concern this man. Crossing the room, she opened the door. "Good night." Her voice was strained. "Thank you for helping him with his soccer."

Gabe hesitated and brushed a thumb over his lips. Then, softly, he said, "Don't give the shoes another thought, Sarah. I'm meeting him for soccer practice tomorrow. I assume you approve? I'll see that he gets home safely, too." Before she could object, he left, pulling the door from her grasp and closing it firmly.

Sarah felt well and truly bulldozed. But by the time she collected her wits and opened the door, he was backing out onto the main road. Of course she would give it another thought! She would sit up half the night juggling bills. She provided for her son, and she didn't need Gabriel Parker making her feel guilty. Tomorrow she'd call the agency, dammit, and tell them Mike didn't need a friend after all.

Slowly she walked to the kitchen and pulled the stack of bills from the drawer. She sat down at the table, spreading them out, sorting them into the order they were due.

"Did Gabe leave, Mom?"

Sarah glanced up and saw the boy standing in the doorway.

"Everything's okay, isn't it?" he asked, his small face etched with worry. "Gabe will meet me tomorrow, won't he?"

Sarah felt as though a huge cauldron was beginning to boil in her stomach. "Go to bed, Mike. Everything's fine." Yet even as she said it, Sarah feared nothing in her life would ever be fine again.

CHAPTER THREE

SARAH OPENED one sleepy eye and tried to unravel the fuzzy threads of a dream. Her bed was shaking. She bolted upright. *A volcano?* No. Not on Oahu. In another moment, she realized the racket was coming from Mike's bedroom.

She grabbed the bedside clock and suppressed an oath. It was late. She'd forgotten to set the alarm.

Shrugging into her robe, she raced down the hall, flung open Mike's door and stopped. The child she normally had to blast out of bed was up and dressed.

"What in the name of heaven are you doing?"

"Jumping rope," he answered.

"I can see that." She put a hand to her brow. "Why?"

"'Cause Gabe said. It builds muscles. Gabe said do it every day."

Sarah closed her mouth, then opened it again. "We're late. Could you fix your lunch while I shower? And that does not mean packing all cookies."

The boy looked insulted. "I gotta eat healthy. Gabe said."

Sarah groaned and turned away. "For once, do what Mom said."

"Hey," he called, "Gabe said I need new soccer shoes."

Sarah paused outside the bathroom door. "And I say we can't afford them this month. Gabe had no right... Oh, this is ridiculous. We're late. Not one more word of wisdom from Gabe Parker until I've had my morning coffee. Understood?"

She entered the bath, cursing Gabe under her breath. When cold water hit her full force, she yelped. Darned faucet needed fixing, too.

The rest of Sarah's morning passed in a blur. Mike missed his bus and she was forced to drive him to school again. As he got out, she reminded him to call if Gabe didn't show. Changing her mind, she said to call either way.

"Okay," he agreed, successfully evading her kiss. "But I wish you'd quit treatin' me like a baby, Mom. I'm goin' on nine, you know."

Sighing, she watched him dash off to meet friends. As she negotiated the heavy traffic, she thought about how hard it was to admit he was growing up. She still hadn't come to grips with it by the time she reached Mitzi's.

"Well?" demanded her friend the moment she slid into the car.

"Sorry to be so late. I forgot to set my alarm."

"I don't mean why are you late. You didn't call to tell me about Gabe Parker." She offered a smug smile. "But Osamu did. Check back issues of the daily paper—Parker's splashed all over the society pages. Women in diamonds. Women in furs. Looks to be more gigolo than community servant."

Sarah pulled her eyes from the traffic. "I'm afraid I don't follow, Mitzi. Are you saying he dates rich older women?"

Mitzi frowned. "Rich, at any rate. His newest conquest is a mere child. Sheena Maxwell. I've heard how much money Layman Maxwell spent on her finishing school in France. Isn't he one of Lou's clients?"

Sarah stopped at Mitzi's corner of Kalia and Ala Moana. "Yes, in fact I think he has an appointment soon. But Sheena isn't exactly a child."

"Oh?" Mitzi lifted a brow. "Mom hadn't read this edition or I would've brought it for you to see. With that mop of hair, Sheena looks just like Farrell's chickie-babe."

Concern crept into Sarah's eyes. "Mr. Maxwell is throwing the do of the year for Sheena's twenty-first birthday. Lou has practically ordered me to attend. I've been trying to get out of it."

"He's big in Rotary, so Osamu was invited, too. Frankly I can't wait."

Sarah drummed her fingers on the steering wheel. "For a while last night, Parker seemed different. Nice. Mike idolizes him. Did Sam say anything specific—about him and Sheena, maybe? Anything I should worry about?"

"Don't get me wrong. My husband thinks the guy walks on water. Knows him from college. Specifically, he told me to butt out." Her eyes grew dark. "I don't want to see your heart stomped on again, Sarah."

When Sarah didn't respond, Mitzi sighed. "Mom's picking me up after work tonight. And she'll drive me in tomorrow. Are we still on for the game?"

"Yes," murmured Sarah. Then before she could steer the conversation back to Mitzi's incorrect assumptions about her interest in Parker, her friend had left the car. Goodness, was anyone else's life so complicated?

Still mulling it over, she angled into her parking slot, got out and slammed the door so hard it rattled the glass. She winced, vowing to forget Gabe Parker and concentrate on work. Upstairs she attacked a backlog of reports left by one of the research assistants.

Harvey invited her to lunch. She begged off and worked straight through. He hadn't been pleased, but it turned out to be for the best. Mitzi's cousin called to say he could take her car the next morning if she paid cash. Sarah thought she might just swing it.

Only after she'd left the bank did her mind return to Gabe Parker. What if he didn't show up for Mike's practice? Maybe she should drop by the field.

"No...no!" she scolded herself aloud. The man in the next car thought she was flirting. With a guilty start, Sarah averted her gaze. But the other side of the highway only reminded her more of Gabe. A frothy surf rolled gently against a brand-new white beach created by one of the big hoteliers. She couldn't remember if the complex belonged to Parker or not. All she knew was that she missed the hibiscus and orchids once bobbing in small neat yards.

Harvey had called it progress. Sarah recalled their ongoing argument. Come to think of it, Maxwell had a hand in, too. He was big in resorts. So, of course, Sheena moved in the same circles as Gabe.

WHEN SHE GOT HOME, the house seemed unnaturally quiet. Instead of using the windfall of free time for herself, Sarah paced and waited for Mike's call. When she still hadn't heard from him by six, she snatched up her car keys and bolted for the door. The shrill ring of the telephone caught her midflight.

Instantly the knot in her stomach unraveled. She raced back across the room to breath an anxious hello into the receiver.

"Hi, Mom!" Hearing Mike's excited voice, Sarah closed her eyes in relief.

"See, I'm calling just like you said. And Mom, Coach said I was better today. He said I'd for sure get to play tomorrow." His voice had a lilt Sarah hadn't heard lately. All at once there was mumbling at Mike's end.

"Gabe says we gotta hurry, Mom. Says to tell you I'll be home in half an hour. 'Bye."

"Wait, Mike—" Sarah wanted a word with Gabe about the shoes, but Mike had hung up. The fact that Parker had shown up should have earned him points with her. Somehow, though, she didn't want to give them. At loose ends, Sarah went to change out of her suit.

She passed a full-length mirror in the hall. She rarely bothered with more than a cursory glance, but this time she stopped to study her image. Solemn brown eyes, neither young nor old, stared back at her. She made a face. She was attractive enough, but no beauty. Never had been and never would be. Thick healthy hair was about her best feature—although Farrell had called it mouse brown. He was forever after her to lighten it, as if he ever left spare money for such things.

Turning away, she bunched what no longer seemed her best feature into a knot and secured it with pins. She'd made a lot of mistakes in her marriage. But she was wiser now.

The roar of an engine outside cut short her assessment. Recognizing it as the Porsche's, Sarah checked her watch. Surely she hadn't been admiring herself for half an hour! No, they were early. Fearing some accident had befallen Mike at practice, she raced for the front door and arrived in a burst of speed, nearly flattening him as he flung it open.

"Are you okay?" She grabbed him around the waist. Before he managed a word, she heard the Porsche rev and retreat. "Wait," she called. "Darn, I needed to talk with him."

"He's gone," Mike said, poking his head outside. "Look what he gave me today." He proudly held aloft a spanking new pair of soccer shoes. "And he told Coach he'd talk to you 'bout soccer camp."

Irrational anger stole Sarah's breath. "I don't believe this," she said the moment her voice returned. "I distinctly told you—"

"I didn't ask or nothin'," he blurted. "Honest. He just brought 'em. And Coach asked him about camp. It wasn't me."

"Well, you can't keep them. For one thing, they must have cost a fortune. And if I can't pay for your camp, young man, you aren't going."

Mike's lower lip trembled. "But I kicked real good today. 'Sides," he pointed out, "I got 'em grass-stained. I don't think Gabe can take 'em back."

"You wore them? Without asking me?" The moment Sarah placed her hands on her hips, he threw the shoes down at her feet and ran to his room.

"You're not fair!" he shouted. "Gabe wants me to kick good. You don't care if I do. You don't care 'bout nothin' but stupid old money."

His accusation rang inside her head. Sarah went into the kitchen and leaned on the counter. Her hands shook. Of course she cared. She wanted him to play well. It was just that she was so angry about the shoes. But why yell at the child? Gabe, now, was an adult. A too-rich irresponsible adult who enjoyed indulging his own whims without regard for the consequences. Just like Farrell had. She should have known.

That evening, Mike refused dinner. Unhappily Sarah noticed that although normally he was quick to forgive, tonight he nursed a grudge. She looked in on him later and found him asleep, hugging his soccer ball and the shoes. Tears had left streaks down his cheeks. Anger at Gabe's insensitivity flared in her breast. Maybe it was time she spelled things out.

Back in her room, Sarah looked up his number in the phone book. *Figures,* she thought, when she didn't find him listed. He probably had to hide from all his little groupies—or their disgruntled husbands.

She flopped down on the bed and massaged her temples. What good would calling do? Mike was right. The shoes were ruined for return. That didn't mean, however, that she intended to let this slide. So much for his saying *she* set the rules. With any luck, by morning Mike would listen to reason.

Unfortunately, the next day the tension between them was even worse. Stony-faced, Mike hopped from the car at a friend's house with only the most perfunctory farewell. The shoes hung brazenly over his shoulder on black-and-white shoestrings. Sarah did her best to ignore them as she issued instructions for after school.

Once she'd left her car at the shop, she thrust the shoe problem from her mind. It was a lovely day, and the short walk to work was rejuvenating. Her peace lasted. Lou was out of town, and Harvey had an early court date.

In the middle of typing a boring brief, it popped into Sarah's mind that she needed to resolve the matter of those soccer shoes once and for all. The agency would surely have a way to reach Gabe. "This is Mrs. Michaels," she greeted the director. "I'd like Gabriel Parker's phone number. Something has come up involving my son."

"It's highly irregular," the man informed her. "It's up to the volunteer to give out his or her phone number." He paused. "I assume this means you've decided to let your son participate in our program?"

Sarah paused. Too late she remembered that she'd never called him back. Faced with a yes or no situation, she could do little but say, "I... ah... yes."

"Is this an emergency? We never give out our volunteers' numbers."

"No," she said, losing steam. "I didn't realize it was against your rules. I'll work something out." Sarah replaced the receiver with a bang. Reaching Parker was tougher than breaking into the U.S. Mint. Well, it would have to wait until tonight's game.

She worked through lunch again and was nearing the end of the last intricate contract when Harvey returned. He stopped, bent for a closer look at her and frowned.

Sarah hit a wrong key, and her screen went blank. "What is it, Harvey? Now I have to start over."

"You look harried, Sarah. Positively rumpled. It isn't like you. Aren't you feeling well?"

Her teeth ground together. She glared up at him through a drooping lock of hair. "I feel fine. I came in early this morning. Sorry if I'm not model-perfect, but it's not as if we're overrun with clients." She struck a series of keys, and a new contract appeared.

"Please go comb your hair and freshen your makeup," he said in prim tones. "I'm due to meet Layman Maxwell for Lou in less than ten minutes. I think you know what an important client he is."

"Well, Harvey, Mr. Maxwell isn't likely to check my makeup. The man looks on me as part of the furniture."

"Don't be difficult. You know our firm is trying to mix socially with clients like the Maxwells. That's why Lou asked us to attend the party they're throwing. I don't want Layman questioning my taste in women."

"I'll pretend you didn't say that," Sarah said tightly. "If I embarrass you, take someone else."

"Of course you don't, Sarah. I only meant—"

But Sarah had snatched her purse out of the drawer and slammed through the outer door toward the ladies' room, effectively cutting off his lame apology. She wasn't doing this because he'd ordered it, but because if she stayed, she might hit him with a dictionary.

Her hand shook as she applied a thin coating of lipstick. Why had she never noticed how dictatorial Harvey was? He hadn't seemed like that when they'd gone out together. Remembering the quiet dinners, the opera, the plays they attended, she felt her anger ebb. She reminded herself that Harvey was a junior partner, and Maxwell was Lou's client. She straightened her blouse and gave one last tug at her skirt before making her way back to the office. The incident with those shoes must have made her extra touchy today.

Through the door's etched glass, Sarah saw that the client had arrived. He stood talking with Harvey. She caught the profile of a slender, elegantly dressed woman beside the two men. As unobtrusively as possible, she tiptoed in and slid behind her desk. Just then, the woman turned and Sarah caught the full force of Sheena Maxwell's flawless beauty.

No wonder Gabe Parker squired her about town. Wide, almost pansy-purple eyes were enhanced by a hint of shadow. Her skin was clear and lightly tanned—just enough to be fashionable. The frothy dress she wore had "original" stamped all over it, and Sarah figured it would pay for at least two car air conditioners. She shifted her attention from the young woman's slightly petulant mouth to an expensive pair of lizard shoes that matched a handbag being twisted impatiently between pink-tipped fingernails.

A sigh escaped Sarah's lips. Was Lou crazy for expecting her to mix with the Maxwell crowd? Nevertheless, in the office part of her job was to entertain Sheena until Harvey completed business with Mr. Maxwell. Sarah couldn't say exactly why she found the prospect so distasteful. Yet it took repeated signals from Harvey to get her moving.

"You're looking exceptionally well, Sheena." Sarah forced a smile. "France obviously agreed with you."

The men rewarded Sarah with grateful glances before walking away.

Sheena's violet eyes lit with pleasure. "Thank you, Miss... Mrs.... Er, do I know you?" She frowned.

Sarah's answer was slow in coming. "Probably not. You were in once or twice with your father a few years back. I don't think you were interested in meeting the office staff. If memory serves, you were impatient to be off playing tennis or sailing."

The young woman aimed an eloquent pout toward Harvey's office. "And so I am today, too. I promised to meet Gabriel at his marina when we got back from Maui. But Daddy absolutely refused to be late for this appointment."

Sheena sat gingerly on the edge of the antique settee, taking care not to wrinkle her dress. "It would have made more sense to drop me off," she confided. "Then he could talk business all afternoon."

At the mention of Gabe's name, Sarah's lips had locked in a false smile. She didn't know why the news annoyed her, especially after Mitzi's revelation. "Would that be Gabriel P-Parker?" Sarah stammered, and then was irked with herself. A cinch Sheena hadn't meant the archangel. Moreover, her question had sounded as if she, Sarah, was personally interested in the man.

"Yes." Sheena looked up from leafing through a trade magazine. "Do you know him?" She sounded shocked. Then the violet eyes narrowed for a moment, carefully assessing Sarah—and, apparently, dismissing her.

Sarah fought the urge to casually say that he'd barbecued hamburgers in her backyard. That would be both petty and childish and she was neither. "Uh, we've met."

Sheena obviously expected some kind of elaboration. As none was forthcoming, she took the initiative. "I assume, *Mr.* Michaels has business dealings with Gabe? He's buying a runabout perhaps?"

"Actually I'm divorced," Sarah stated flatly.

When Sheena blanched under her perfect tan, Sarah couldn't believe she'd been deliberately evasive. More than evasive—inflammatory.

"Just how well do you know him?" demanded the younger woman, dropping all pretense of reading the business journal.

What was she doing? Those two deserved each other, and she had never intentionally caused problems for any of Lou's clients. Sarah grabbed up a stack of contracts that needed signatures and headed for Lou's office.

"Well?" Sheena tapped her toe impatiently.

"I met him through my son's soccer." That was the truth, Sarah told herself as she moved to close Lou's private door.

"Is that all," sniffed Sheena, before the door actually shut. "I knew you weren't his type. Say, could I use your telephone? It just occurred to me that Gabriel may as well come here to pick me up. That way it'll give us more than just this evening together."

"Be my guest." Sarah stuck her head back out into the office. "Push nine for an outside line." Retreating, she let the door slam. *Not his type, indeed.* As if she'd want to be a surf queen. Then she wondered how Sheena fit in with the surfing crowd. It was hard picturing her with sand under those fingernails.

Sarah smacked the stack of reports down on Lou's desk. His desk clock bounced. She righted it and saw the time. Four-twenty. Yikes! She'd planned to pick up her car, get Mitzi and still get to Mike's game early.

That was when it struck her. Sheena had clearly indicated she had a date with Gabe, yet he'd promised to be at Mike's game. Anger set her stomach churning. She marched out, breezed past the woman still chatting on *her* phone and snapped off her computer. "I'm leaving," she announced at large.

Sheena ignored her. Turning her back, she lowered her voice and giggled, saying, "Oh, Gabriel, you're such a tease."

Head held high, Sarah left the building. She'd be darned if she'd give Mike excuses for dear *Gabriel*. Of course he'd be disappointed—at first. But she and Mitzi would be there to support him. Somehow, Sarah found it comforting to know nothing had changed, after all.

Resolutely she entered the shop to collect her car. The good news was that it cost fifty dollars less than the estimate. On the way to pick up Mitzi, she basked in the cooler air. Tonight, she'd spring for the largest gooiest pizza Arnold's offered. She actually laughed.

"Better day?" Mitzi greeted her as she climbed in. "Mine was horrible. Oh, Lord, this air is heavenly. Sarah," she squealed, "you got it fixed!"

An answering grin brought out the dimples in Sarah's cheeks. "Plus, your cousin saved me money on the repair. Win or lose tonight, the pizza's my treat."

"Shouldn't you buy Mike new soccer shoes, instead?" Mitzi turned in the seat. "I mean, if Parker was right."

"He already bought Mike shoes. It's been a hot topic at our house. Mike wore them without asking me." She frowned. "But you're right, Mitzi, I'll have to pay him back. I should have thought of that."

"Oh, I don't know." Mitzi's expression was thoughtful. "He can certainly afford a lousy pair of shoes. And maybe it's part of the Island Child program. Did you ask?"

"He would have said. He knew how I felt. I intended to have it out with him tonight, but when I left the office, Sheena Maxwell was on the phone arranging their date. I'm sure he won't be at the game. And I don't relish breaking that news to Mike."

"He wouldn't do that after promising, would he?" Mitzi looked aghast. "Even I know how important follow-through is with kids."

"Could we talk about something else? Anyway, you didn't see Sheena. She's very beautiful and, I imagine, very persuasive. Are you spending the night at our place?"

"She's also *very* young for your Mr. Parker," Mitzi said, ignoring Sarah's attempt to change the subject.

Sarah didn't respond, and Mitzi sighed. "I have pj's and a sweat suit in this suitcase I call a purse. No sense driving me home. Especially with Sam away."

The two women talked little after that. At Sarah's, they changed clothes and hurried to the field. Sarah had hoped to catch Mike with friends—to make telling him easier. But the moment they pulled in, she saw him waiting.

Mitzi reached over and clasped her arm. "Do you want me to stay while you break the bad news, or should I go find us a seat?"

"You go ahead. Try for midway up the bleachers. I'll be along. Lordy, I don't want to do this."

Mitzi narrowed her eyes. "Parker is dead meat. Wait till I tell Sam." She withdrew, pausing a moment to chat with Mike.

Sarah was slow to leave the car.

"Hurry, Mom!" the child called. "I gotta get back to the team. Why are you late? And where's Gabe, do you 'spose?"

Sarah took one look at his bright happy face and wished she could get her hands on Parker's neck. "My, but you guys look handsome with matching shirts," she said, hugging him compulsively. "So grown-up." Her voice cracked.

"Aw, Mom. Don't do that. The guys might see." Deftly he sidestepped and bounced up on his toes, peering into the gathering dusk.

"Mike," Sarah said firmly, "I hate to tell you this—" she swallowed a lump "—but I don't think Gabe'll make your game tonight."

He stopped bouncing. "'Course he will. He promised." Then when her solemn expression didn't change, his face crumpled.

"Oh, honey." She wanted to hug him again even though he'd warned her off. Her heart ached for him.

"I don't believe you," he said, his voice rising. "Gabe promised, Mom. He promised!"

"What's going on here, kicker?"

Sarah jerked around. Shocked, her eyes met Gabe Parker's cool blue gaze. He knelt to Mike's level, and Sarah was forced to watch her son throw himself into her enemy's arms. She couldn't think straight, couldn't breathe.

"She said you weren't coming to my game." Mike buried his head in Gabe's broad shoulder. "And I said you promised." Like magic, the child's sniffles subsided.

Gabe's brow arched. "Why would you lie to him?"

"Now, just a darn minute—" Sarah prepared to defend herself.

"So this is what you meant when you said you knew Gabriel." The lilting voice came from behind Sarah. She whirled again.

"You didn't say your son was his community service project." Sheena Maxwell's cultured tone held the barest hint of amusement.

Sarah took in all of Sheena's pristine white silk pantsuit before she snarled, "My son is no one's service project." Furious, she turned to Gabe. "We do not need charity, Mr. Parker. Which brings me to the subject of soccer shoes. I told you *I'd* get them." Digging in her purse, she pulled out her fifty dollars, and although she could ill afford the gesture, she smacked it into his hand. "There. Why don't you trot on back to the high-rent district where you belong? I'll be paying for his soccer camp, too."

"Yippee!" Mike gave a whoop.

Gabe stood, lifting the happy child into his arms. He shoved the bills back in Sarah's purse. "I don't understand any of this. The shoes were a gift. I didn't realize there was any question about my attending his game. And Coach asked if I'd discuss camp with you." He paused a moment, cocking an ear. "The preliminary whistle just blew. Could we sort this out later?"

Sarah's face remained mutinous.

Mike tugged Gabe's chin around. "You said you'd sit with the team. Are you still gonna do that?"

"You bet I am, kicker." Gabe smiled.

"What about me?" Sheena protested as Mike slid to the ground and the two started walking away.

Gabe turned, his face a mask of surprise. "You asked to come. Go with Sarah. That way you'll be rooting for the right team." He left the two women glaring daggers at one another.

Sarah swept past Sheena. Gabe's little playmate could follow or not. When she was stopped by a mother collecting a nominal fee to help defray the cost of full uniforms only to learn that Gabe had already paid for her *and* Sheena, Sarah was livid. If he thought he could treat her like one of his surf bunnies, he'd better think again.

Stalking away, Sarah scanned the bleachers for Mitzi. Once she'd located her, she made her way up, then flung herself down on the hard bench. She staved off the other woman's questions with a curt, "Don't even ask."

"Wow," Mitzi said. "Who's that? Get a load of the white suit. Is she for real? White at a kids' soccer game! Who'd be that stupid?"

"French silk, I'd bet," said Sarah tartly. "*That,* is Sheena Maxwell. She's with Parker."

"You mean he's here? No kidding? Where?" Mitzi craned her neck. "And I thought you were upset because of Mike."

"I am." Sarah lowered her voice. "Could we go into this later? People are listening."

A chubby boy dressed in a T-shirt that matched Mike's stepped on Sarah's toes as he scrambled past.

"Hello, Mr. and Mrs. Cline." Sarah nodded to the parents of Mike's school friend, Jim, who were seated on Mitzi's right.

"Glad you could make the game, Mrs. Michaels." An older balding version of the son smiled at her. Then his wife chimed in, "We were just discussing you, Sarah. Is Mike's father back in town?"

Sarah nearly dropped her teeth. "No. Ah, the man is just a friend. *Mike's* friend," she added needlessly, then felt her cheeks grow warm.

"Really?" Mrs. Cline's eyebrows shot up.

"I get your drift now, Sarah," Mitzi whispered.

Sarah focused on the team. Mike's resemblance to Gabe was uncanny. It wasn't hard to see what Mrs. Cline was thinking.

Mitzi whistled long and low. "So that's Parker? I can tell you the pictures in the paper don't do him justice. He's *beautiful.*"

"Mitzi!" Sarah might have said more, but a hush fell over the crowd as everyone stood for the presentation of the flag, which signaled the start of the game. The moment the pledge ended, Sarah sat. It bothered her to be looking down on Gabe's broad back, so she studied the crowd, instead. There was a good turnout. But throughout the first quarter, her eyes strayed often to the ripple of muscles playing beneath Gabe's white shirt. Unlike Sheena, who was sitting beside him, he fit right in with the casual crowd. Sarah's pulse sped up just watching him.

Mitzi poked her and cheered as Mike's team scored a point. Guiltily Sarah straightened and tried to concentrate on the game.

Suddenly it was halftime. Mike hadn't been off the bench. Sarah didn't want to go to the concession stand, but Mitzi propelled her forward. Did all parents agonize over their children's feelings the way she did? Sarah wondered. For an unguarded moment she watched Gabe talking quietly with her son. Was it wrong to be relieved that someone else was consoling him for a change? An inner voice cautioned, *Don't depend on Parker too much.*

Mike caught sight of her and yelled, "Coach says I get to play the second half. And, Mom, I invited Gabe for pizza. That's okay, isn't it?"

Sarah glanced from Gabe to Sheena, who had suddenly appeared at his side. "Maybe another time. Tonight's family. Besides, I'm sure Gabe has other plans."

Gabe kept silent as he lifted Mike and swung him in the air. The child giggled, and Sarah's heart twisted convulsively.

"Aunt Mitzi isn't real family," Mike said.

Belatedly remembering her manners, Sarah introduced Mitzi.

Gabe, in turn, did the same with Sheena.

Sarah almost laughed, thinking how amiable they must seem to others.

"Well, can he?" Mike pressed.

"Oh, we couldn't possibly," Sheena answered for them. "Gabriel is taking me to dinner at the club."

Sarah felt relieved. Although she'd never been to the country club, she knew it was a far cry from Arnold's Pizzeria.

Gabe laughed and said to Mike, "Women go for atmosphere, kicker." Turning to Sheena, he said lightly, "I only promised food. Pizza's food."

"All right!" Mike jumped up and down. "So is it okay, huh, Mom?"

"Of course they're welcome," Sarah agreed stiffly. "But Arnold's doesn't have atmosphere."

"Does so," Mitzi interjected. "They have tablecloths and candles."

"There you go." Gabe winked at the now glowering Sheena.

Before Sarah could mention that Arnold's table coverings were oilcloth and their candles the drip kind stuffed into cheap wine bottles, the call to play sent them all scurrying for their seats.

"Latch on to that guy, Sarah," murmured Mitzi near her ear. "Mike adores him and vice versa. Plus, he's got a beautiful bod."

"Mitzi Kealoha," Sarah sputtered. "It's out of the question. We'd kill each other first."

"Too bad. Oh, hey," Mitzi grabbed Sarah's arm. "Mike's going out to play." Clinging to one another, they stopped and took seats where they were. In spite of the balmy night, Sarah shivered as she watched her son join the fracas. She did want him to play, but...sometimes players got hurt. Quite by accident, her anxious gaze locked with Gabe's.

Casually he left Sheena and moved up the aisle to sit beside her. He placed a broad comforting hand on her shoulder. "First-game jitters, huh, Mom? Mike's doing fine."

She breathed in the scent of his expensive after-shave and felt her heartbeat quicken. He smiled then, and Sarah saw confidence in her son reflected in that smile. It was crazy how her pulse leapt again.

"What do you suppose Mrs. Cline's thinking now?" Mitzi asked in a low amused voice.

Sarah looked guilty and slid out from under Gabe's hand.

Seemingly oblivious of the undercurrent—and of Sheena's pout—he remained at Sarah's side, shouting encouragement to the players until the whistle blew and it was formally declared that Mike's team had lost by one point. Then he rushed out to meet the team, leaving all three women behind. They filed after him in silence, reaching ground level as a dejected Mike shuffled off the field.

Gabe clapped him on the shoulder. "No dishonor in losing when you play a good game. How would you like a ride to Arnold's in my Porsche?"

"Really?" Mike's demeanor changed. "Can I, Mom?" he asked.

As though sensing her hesitation, Mitzi piped up with, "Such a deal, kid. I'm jealous. We'll meet ya. First one there gets the table. We'll have a good time. Right, Sarah?" She started hustling Sarah away.

Sarah blinked. Why was it she lost all control whenever Gabe Parker was around? For Mike's sake, she needed to make an effort to be more congenial. "That's right," she called back. "We're going to have fun."

She meant it, too, until she was stuffed in a too-small booth next to Gabe and Sheena. Sarah gave up all pretense of congeniality and simply held her tongue until Gabe snapped up the bill. Sarah insisted it was her treat. But he already had his money out.

Mitzi silenced her with a kick under the table.

Sarah gave in gracefully, making a mental note to settle with him in private.

Outside, she lost no time saying good-night. Mike protested, but she was firm. "Mike, you've claimed enough of Gabe's attention. He and Sheena still have time to go to the club." At that, the woman in white actually aimed a stiff smile her way. Gabe, though, didn't seem in any rush to leave.

"We'll see," he said, lifting Mike, who was trying hard not to yawn. Carrying him to Sarah's car, Gabe tucked him carefully into the back seat.

"Thanks," Sarah said, grateful for his help. "He's getting to be a chunk, I'm afraid."

Gabe straightened, concern in his expression. "I could follow you home and lift him out at the other end. He'll be good and zonked by then."

Sarah stopped digging for her keys. She gave him a blank look.

Sheena called to him from the Porsche, but Gabe leaned an arm along the top of Sarah's car. "Would it be okay if Mike helps out on my boat tomorrow? I promised him I'd ask. I'll come pick him up about ten."

"Absolutely not," Sarah hissed. "Shh. I don't want him to hear you."

"Oh, please, Mom!" Mike's eyes flew open. "You said he hadda ask first. So he did."

Visions of Farrell's wild beach parties swam before Sarah's eyes. Stubbornly she shook her head. "I don't like boats," she said at last.

"Mine is docked for repairs." Gabe smiled. Privately he wondered what she had against boats. There seemed to be an awful lot she didn't like. Sometime—later, when she trusted him more—he'd ask her some questions. . . .

"He's not you-know-who," Mitzi was murmuring in her other ear.

Sarah slid behind the steering wheel. "I wouldn't want Mike to get in any workman's way."

"If that was the case, I wouldn't have asked," Gabe said. "Don't tell me you couldn't use a little time to yourself."

Time to herself? A rare commodity. A tiny smile crept in. Still, the feeling that she needed to protect herself and her son from some unnamed threat was stronger than the appeal of a few private hours. "Uh..."

Mitzi butted in. "You deserve a break," she said. "But I warn you—" she nudged Gabe "—she'll grow to like it." Taking charge, Mitzi shooed him away, saying, "I'm spending the night with Sarah. Since I live on the way to your marina, you can give me a lift home in the morning. Sarah won't even have to leave the house."

"Now look what you've done," Sarah whispered as Mike came awake again long enough to clap gleefully. "And Sheena looks ready to kill you," Sarah added, watching Gabe climb in the Porsche and drive off.

"Really?" Mitzi drawled. "I was just thinking what a sport ol' Sheena was being, too."

Sarah shot her friend a sidelong glance. A devilish smile hovered on Mitzi's lips. Sarah dissolved in laughter. "I swear, Mitzi, you'd make a good politician. How do you lie with a straight face?"

"Is that any way to treat someone who got you a morning of freedom?"

"Freedom?" Sarah sobered and glanced at her sleeping son. "I don't think so. Mitzi, I'm scared. Haven't you noticed that Gabe Parker is... is stealing Mike's affections?"

"Mike loves you, Sarah," Mitzi insisted. "Nothing can change that."

"I guess I don't have your faith, Mitzi," Sarah said unhappily. "Right now, I wish I'd never signed him up for that stupid program."

CHAPTER FOUR

EVERYONE IN THE MICHAELS household slept late the next morning. When they did awaken, Mike was so excited Sarah noticed he brushed his teeth three times—without once being told. And yet, some part of her didn't want to let him go.

"He'll be all right, Sarah." Mitzi sighed as she watched her friend keeping a nervous eye on the clock. "Just what do you think can happen to him on a boat docked on dry land?"

Sarah chewed at her lip, her habitual expression of worry. "I don't know how to explain it. Weekends have been our special time together since he was born. It's harder sharing him than I ever imagined it would be."

Mitzi finished her coffee and rinsed the cup. "I'm sure those child-care books of yours have a paragraph or two on letting go. What if you remarry? Have more children?"

Sarah was mildly surprised at Mitzi's attitude. "It's not like I'm being one of those smother-mothers," she said defensively.

"I'm not accusing you," Mitzi assured. "It's just, well, I don't want you to forget you have a life of your own. Mike'll get married one of these days and leave home. Then where will you be?"

Sarah rolled her eyes. "He's only eight years old, Mitzi." She would have said more, but was interrupted by Gabe's arrival and Mike's effusive shout from the living room.

"He's here, Mom. Gabe's here. Hurry, Aunt Mitzi. We don't wanna keep him waiting. 'Bye, Mom. See you later."

The front door opened, then banged shut.

Sarah's mouth gaped, and Mitzi laughed.

"He's not excited or anything," Mitzi said dryly. "Do you want to come wave goodbye, or should I just leave quietly?"

Sarah followed Mitzi to the door. Mike was already belted into the jump seat, urging Mitzi to hurry. A stab of jealousy knifed through Sarah's heart. Once again, she couldn't help feeling that Gabe was replacing her in her son's affections.

"See you later," called Gabe. "Enjoy yourself." He grinned, waved to her and started backing out the moment Mitzi was settled in the passenger seat. Those two chatted like old friends.

Today, Sarah noticed, Gabe's electric-blue eyes were hidden by mirrored sunglasses. One suntanned arm rested casually out his window.

"'Bye." Mike twisted on his perch, stuck an arm out the window behind Gabe's head and flopped his hand like a dead fish. Suddenly Sarah was struck by envy. Was *that* what this was all about? Surely not. She had never wanted to go with Farrell. Maybe if she had... but no, she'd never had time to play. There was always so much to do around the house.

Sarah remained on the porch until the car disappeared from view. Then it hit her that she'd failed to ask Gabe for a telephone number—again. Come to think of it, she hadn't even asked when they'd return. What kind of mother was she? A little smile came and went. The way Mike talked nonstop, he'd soon drive Gabe crazy. No doubt she'd see them back before lunch. Time for herself, indeed. In fact, she'd better work fast to get everything done.

But noon came, and they hadn't returned. Sarah collapsed with a cup of leftover breakfast coffee and wondered how Gabe was faring. She'd finished the wash, changed all the beds, cleaned up the mess in Mike's room and scrubbed the bathroom floor. Any minute now they'd walk in.

She checked her watch. Did she have time for a shower? Moments ago she'd caught a glimpse of herself in one of the mirrors. Her hair was frightful, poking willy-nilly out from beneath a hastily tied scarf. Plus, she had several black smudges on her face.

What would Gabe think if he saw her looking like Cinderella before the ball? He probably believed all women dressed like Sheena. She found herself picturing his family. He'd mentioned his father, but what was his mother like? Frivolous, or athletic?

When the duo didn't arrive within the next ten minutes, Sarah rose, dumped her coffee and peered out the window. She unloaded the dishwasher, keeping one ear tuned for the whine of the Porsche.

As she cleaned counters, Sarah had a new thought about how to reach Gabe. She leafed through the Yellow Pages, looking for marinas. Parker's was listed in bold type, and she felt a moment of triumph. Triumph soon gone sour, as she reached a recorded message informing her that all sales staff were out helping customers at the moment. Leave a name and number, the message told her, and someone would call her back. Sarah hung up.

She decided to scrub her oven next. Since it wasn't the self-cleaning type, this was a chore she normally saved until a pie bubbled over. The inside and both racks sparkled before she tried the marina again. By this time three of her fingernails had ragged edges. Irrationally she blamed Gabe. If he'd been as responsible as the agency said, he'd have told her what time they'd be back.

"Parker Boat and Marina," a sweet voice trilled over the line.

"My name is Sarah Michaels," she said without explanation. "I'm calling Gabriel Parker. Could you transfer me or give me a number where he can be reached?" Since she'd made an effort to keep her tone professional, the silence at the other end surprised her. Sarah repeated her request with less patience.

"I'm sorry," the woman said. "Mr. Parker is not available on weekends."

"But you don't understand," Sarah said. "My son's with him on his boat. I expected them back before now."

"I really can't give out his private number. Now if you'll excuse me, I have another call coming in."

A click and soft hum sounded before Sarah could explain further. "Blast." She slammed down the receiver. Did that woman think she wanted Gabe for *personal* reasons? Sarah realized it was probably exactly what she thought.

Feeling a sudden need for fresh air, she went outside and set about pruning hibiscus that hadn't felt a blade in two years. She swiveled toward the road each time she heard a car until it seemed her head would split.

After the flower beds were tidy, Sarah washed windows—another dirty job that matched her mood. If they didn't arrive soon, she was going to call the police. Although just what she'd say wasn't clear in her mind. She could hardly report the man for kidnapping, could she?

By five o'clock, Sarah was not only exhausted, she was frantic. She abandoned all pretext of work and paced from window to window, her head throbbing like a war drum. All sorts of wild possibilities flitted about inside her head. Mike had fallen from the boat. Gabe had been in a wreck and they were in some emergency room, unconscious. He'd gone to some beach party and forgotten Mike altogether. Not once did she think they might simply be having such a good time that the hours slipped away.

Once she gave up and just sat, Sarah dozed off and missed the muffled whine of the Porsche when it finally did arrive. The house was dark.

Mike exploded through the front door and hit the lights, catapulting his mother from her chair.

One look at her grimy face and the boy stopped his excited dialogue about the boat. "Gee," he observed, "Mom looks like that rose again, don't she, Gabe?"

Under the harsh overhead lights, Gabe appeared so much her opposite—calm and cool in his white shorts and bright yellow tank top—that something in Sarah snapped. Catching Mike to her roughly, she demanded, "Where have you been? Do you have any idea how worried I've been? Why didn't you call?"

Her outburst took Gabe by surprise, but he knew her well enough by now to tread lightly, even though he still wasn't certain why her soft brown eyes were always guarded. The agency application had revealed nothing, and this morning Mitzi Kealoha had been hesitant to talk about her friend. Over the course of the day he had learned from Mike that there were no grandparents, that there was a father who never sent so much as a birthday card and that Sarah was often too tired to have fun.

Mike tore free from his mother's grasp and ran to Gabe. He threw his arms about the man's waist. "Gabe and me had fun today!" he cried.

Gabe reached behind him and closed the door. "What Mike did on my boat was work, Sarah. He waxed the railings and helped clean the galley cupboards. It wasn't all play," he said in a reasonable tone.

"It was fun," Mike insisted. "I got to run up the sail, and Gabe and me fished off the dock. Sheena came by. Wow, Mom! You oughtta see her bathin' suit. It was neat-o."

Gabe tried to explain. "It was the color. He likes hot pink. She was on her way to Morgan Tate's pool party. I think Mike wanted us to go."

Sarah pulled the boy back. "That would be foolish. He doesn't know how to swim."

"Gabe said he'd teach me," Mike said, stamping a foot. "Someday, I'm gonna find my dad's boat. I bet he wouldn't make me call home, neither." He turned, about to flee the room.

Gabe blocked his path. "I think you owe your mother an apology, kicker. I gave you telephone numbers the other day. Did you forget to pass them on?"

Mike hung his head. "Yeah," he mumbled. "I'm sorry, Mom."

Sarah smoothed a drooping lock of hair out of her eyes with a trembling hand. "Go get cleaned up. You and I will discuss this later."

The child looked subdued. "Gabe was gonna take us out for hamburgers. Does this mean we don't get to go?"

Gabe moved to the center of the room. He would have tried to reason with Sarah if he hadn't gained a closer look at her pallid face, her stricken eyes. "Why don't you go wash your hands, Mike?" he suggested quietly. "Give me a minute with your mom. If we don't go for burgers tonight, we'll do it another time."

"But, Gabe—"

"Go on. Scoot, or we won't go next time, either."

"Yes, sir." The boy shuffled his feet and frowned, but he went without another word. Sarah didn't notice that Gabe stepped closer and blocked the bright light from her eyes.

"Sarah, what's wrong?" With gentle hands, he turned her rigid body toward his taller frame.

Suddenly her whole body began to shake. "Do you see what you've done? Mike has never ever mentioned finding Farrell. He's always been content! Until now."

Without a care for his clean shirt, Gabe pressed her smudged face into the cradle of his shoulder and held her tightly until the shudders coursing through her began to subside. All the while, he murmured soothing words, gently rocking her. "I doubt Mike meant a word of that. It's just, well, he was so excited about his day. I don't think he was prepared for your anger. You know how kids are. It was his way of striking back."

Sarah struggled for release and he let her go immediately.

"I'm sorry," she said stiffly. "I don't normally fall apart like this. I'm tired, and I was so worried." She began to rub her upper arms.

"I'm not surprised you're tired." Gabe replaced her hands with his own and slowly massaged warmth into her icy skin. He frowned down into her eyes. "This time today was for you, Sarah—to pamper yourself. Instead, you cleaned all day. The house sparkles. As we drove in, I noticed all the shrubs had been trimmed and the flower beds weeded. Ye gods, woman! I've known some compulsive people, but..." He loosened his grip and tried to get a smile out of her.

"If your idea of pampering is polishing boats, finding a good wave and having a bevy of pretty women on shore to stroke your ego, then save your lecture." She took a deep breath and clasped her hands tight to keep them from shaking. "Please leave. You've done enough for one day."

His eyes flashed, then cooled. "Are you quite finished? I happen to be on vacation, which you would have known if you'd read the letter from the agency. And if you'd looked at your packet and studied the mission statement, you'd see our purpose is twofold—to provide a child one-on-one time with his or her friend *and* to give the parent a break. Now go sit down. Put your feet up and think about what I said for five minutes. I'll fix us some coffee. Afterward, Mike and I'll go out and grab something to eat while you shower." With a broad sweep of his arm, he picked Sarah up and deposited her none too gently in a high-backed recliner, then yanked up the footrest in a move that dared her to object.

She didn't. She simply stared, openmouthed.

Satisfied, Gabe spun on his heel and disappeared into the kitchen. Damn, but she was a stubborn frustrating woman. Why did he bother?

Part of Sarah wanted to end things here and now. Another part felt foolish, guilty, remorseful. Why did she become so irrational around Gabe? Closing her eyes, Sarah experienced a rush of shame. How could she tell him that she didn't know how to accept pampering? That she was afraid of history repeating itself? And therein, she supposed, lay the real problem. He awakened feelings in her she didn't want awakened.

When Gabe returned with a steaming mug of coffee, Sarah was curled up and sleeping like a kitten. Seeing her softened by sleep, he was struck by a sudden urge to kiss her awake. He recalled how nice it had felt to hold her. Coffee slopped over the mug's rim. He bit back an oath just as Mike dashed into the room.

The boy's face was freshly scrubbed and his blond hair clung damply to his forehead. Gabe put a finger to his lips. Mike nodded. "I know why she's tired," he whispered loudly. "You should see my bedroom. She squeaked it clean."

Gabe smiled. "She squeaked a lot clean today, kicker. What do you say—shall we surprise her and fix dinner? I think we owe her, don't you?"

Mike stood there, considering.

Gabe thought perhaps he was expecting a lot. He knew how badly the child wanted to go for hamburgers. Yet it was important that he learn to give and not just take, to show consideration for others.

The low rumble of their voices nudged Sarah awake. From beneath sleepy lashes she saw how her son looked at Gabe. She ached at the way he wore his heart on his sleeve—more fragile than she'd ever imagined.

"I guess it's my fault she's mad," the boy conceded after a moment's deliberation. "I should've give her the phone numbers. So let's fix dinner."

Gabe set Sarah's cup on the low table and squeezed the boy's shoulder. "Good choice, my man. But you don't deserve all the blame. Next time, we'll communicate better before we leave." Silently they tiptoed out.

Sarah yawned and stretched.

After a while, she dredged up enough energy to leave the chair. Although she was relieved to have Mike home, those ambivalent feelings she held about Gabe Parker left her mind jumbled.

Only Mike's earlier comment regarding the way she looked drove her to more than a quick shower. A hot bath was in order. While water ran in the tub, she shed her grungy jeans. Every muscle protested. Sighing, she slipped into the steaming water and leaned back. And she dawdled, thinking Gabe would get tired of waiting and leave. She couldn't hear them—perhaps he had. It was too quiet. In that case, she'd better get out. Eight-year-old boys could get into a lot of trouble if left alone. Quickly she pulled the plug.

Her work in the yard had given her skin a golden hue. The green silk blouse she selected to wear complimented her heightened skin tone and brought out the gold flecks in her brown eyes. Shorts would be cooler, but what if Gabe was still here? Self-conscious, she donned a pair of well-washed jeans, instead.

Mike's radio had begun blaring from his room. Enticing aromas wafted from the kitchen, more or less confirming that she hadn't outwaited Gabe. Sarah hadn't thought herself hungry, but now she was famished.

She paused at the door to the kitchen and watched him efficiently tend various bubbling pots on the stove. Gabe seemed at ease with a dish towel draped carelessly about his lean hips to serve as an apron. Her heart did a funny tumble in her chest. The two men she'd known best, her father and Farrell, had deemed the kitchen women's territory. Neither would have been caught dead behind a stove, to say nothing of wearing an apron.

"Hello," she said, once the surprise had passed. "Are you single-handedly responsible for all these mouth-watering smells?"

Gabe turned with a broad smile, which quickly changed into a long low whistle of approval. "My, what magic there is in a little soap and water." He brandished a spoon. "Mike said you like spaghetti. It's quick and easy, and it goes with the red wine I grabbed on the way here. Mike got a soft drink. I trust that's okay."

Sarah pushed herself away from the door frame and peeked into a bubbling pot of sauce. "Mmm. Heavenly. I *love* spaghetti. So you're a gourmet cook?"

Even white teeth gleamed from Gabe's tanned face as he threw back his head and laughed. "I'd hardly call boxed spaghetti and canned sauce gourmet cooking, Sarah. But I'm relieved Mike didn't just talk me into fixing it because it was *his* favorite, next to hamburgers."

Sarah watched his strong throat as he laughed. Her gaze shifted to the springy tuft of hair showing above the scooped neck of his snug tank top. Unconsciously she wet her lips and looked away. She felt . . . dizzy.

Gabe's eyes locked on the small sweep of her tongue. He closed the distance between them until he could actually feel her tremble. He wanted so badly to kiss her. But before their lips touched, the shrill screech of the stove's timer broke them apart. With a guilty start, Gabe turned to check a steaming pot. "Break out the wine, woman!" he said in a husky tone. "That dreadful noise means our dinner's ready." Was he crazy? Kissing her would complicate everything.

Sarah was glad of the opportunity to busy her hands. Furtive glances showed Gabe calmly draining the spaghetti noodles. Sure that her own cheeks matched the dark red of the wine, Sarah found herself resenting the fact that he seemed undisturbed. "I'll get Mike," she said, nerves frayed. "He should be helping."

"He did set the table, buttered the French bread and put it in the oven," Gabe said. "I didn't want something boiling over on him."

"I'm not accusing you of anything," she said, lifting a brow.

"It'd be the first time, then," he muttered as she left the room.

It occurred to Sarah that Gabe might not be so unaffected by her, after all.

Mike was lying on his bed, out like a light. When she tried rousing him, he only mumbled and rolled over. After several attempts, Sarah gave up. She'd keep a plate warm in case he woke up later. Although she didn't like the idea of sharing an intimate dinner with Gabe Parker, she didn't think it fair to let his culinary efforts go to waste.

"Can you believe that munchkin fell asleep?" she said lightly as she entered the dining nook and Gabe looked expectantly behind her.

"Do you want me to try waking him?" He set his napkin aside and began to rise.

She shook her head. "I've learned to let sleeping bears lie."

He smiled and assisted her into the nook with its built-in bench seat against the wall. Then he lifted his glass of wine in a toast. "To uneventful hibernations."

She laughed, touching her glass to his. "You know, you make it darned hard on a woman to stay mad. I intended to duke it out with you over several things, not the least of which is making me go gray from worry." She held out a few strands of sleek brown hair, not a gray one in sight.

"I'm sorry, Sarah," he said simply. "Mike seemed to be having a good time. It never entered my mind that you wouldn't jump at the chance for extra hours. Forgive me?" He decided it was best to lay all his cards on the table. "You don't look any the worse for it now." He raised his glass to toast her again, his gaze frank and admiring.

Sarah was reminded anew how much his eyes resembled Mike's—especially when he'd been naughty and knew it. However, the lips touching the wine glass were not those of an eight-year-old. They were the firm mobile lips of a man. Seeing the way they caressed the frosted crystal sent unexpected shivers up her spine.

She shifted on the bench and turned her own glass by its stem. Farrell had been quick to beg her forgiveness, too. But his apologies were nothing more than a means to get his own way. "Let's eat before this gets cold," she said crisply.

Tension was back thick in the air. This time, Gabe sensed it had little to do with him. At least he hoped that was the case. Yet he didn't want a repeat of today. He pulled out his billfold and removed a business card. He got up quickly to to retrieve a pen he'd noticed on the little desk in the hall and scribbled on the back of the card. Then he pushed it across the table.

"I don't want you worrying," he said. "I've listed all the numbers where I might be. The marina, my apartment, my parents' home and the beach house at Sunset. Although I'm not competing in the Grand National Surfing Championship this year, they've asked me to judge. Qualifying starts in a couple of weeks. I'll be taking another week of vacation, so I'll be at Sunset Beach a lot."

He glanced up and caught a flash of something he couldn't quite identify in her eyes. "Maybe you'd like to come for the finals," he offered. "It's over a weekend. Mike would have a blast. And a couple of days in the sun would do you good. What do you say?"

"No!" Her fork slipped through her fingers and crashed against her plate. "And you can forget taking Mike to your boat again. It's not an environment I want to encourage."

Puzzled, Gabe countered, "What kind of environment do you think it is, Sarah? I don't have wild parties or sex orgies. My friends and staff are clean-cut decent people."

"Really?" Sarah gave a careless toss of her head. "What about Sheena's hot-pink bathing suit? I know what sells boats—women draped all over them in sailor hats and string bikinis."

Despite his better intentions, Gabe's gaze slid from her lips to the pulse pounding at the base of her throat—then lower to the open V of her silk shirt. "I don't employ bikini-clad women. My grandfather built a craft that sold on its own merit. I do likewise." He leaned toward her, an elbow on the table. "Out of curiosity, Sarah, what kind of suit do *you* wear swimming?"

"I don't," she said, still processing what he'd just said. Then, when his eyes widened and she realized how her reply sounded, she sat up straight. "I mean, I don't have time to waste swimming."

He smiled a lazy smile. "I like the first notion better."

Even though Sarah wanted to be indignant, her body had other ideas. No one had assessed her this thoroughly as a woman in a very long time—if ever. Her pulse leapt. "Don't," she said, flustered. "Why are you staring at me?"

"Incredible." Gabe shook his head. "People travel thousands of miles to enjoy our beaches, and you're telling me you and Mike don't go. I don't understand why not, but it does explain his preoccupation with swimsuits."

"That is precisely what I want to avoid." Her hands balled into fists.

"The truth is, Sarah, that he's at the age when boys start looking at pictures of women and they speculate."

"At eight?" She sounded shocked. She *was* shocked.

"Eight or eighty, Sarah. It's normal." His eyes strayed to her blouse again. A wry smile played at one corner of his mouth as he looked away and ran a finger around the rim of his wineglass. "Believe me, it's normal."

Suddenly everything Sarah kept bottled inside—the fear that Mike would turn out like his father erupted. "I signed Mike up for Befriend an Island Child because I wanted him to learn life doesn't begin and end at the beach. I had hoped he'd see women being treated with respect, tenderness and love." She hesitated, realizing her own desires were spilling into this conversation.

Gabe chewed and swallowed the bite he'd taken. Then he pushed his plate aside and leaned forward, confronting her. "Respect, tenderness and love begin at home, Sarah. *You* have to be his role model, his example. What kind of messages are you sending him?" At once he felt like a rat because her face fell and her eyes looked terribly sad. Damn! Something about that look drew his sympathy.

Tiny, strangled protests lay trapped in Sarah's throat. She crushed her napkin and her hand brushed her wineglass. It toppled. Tearing her gaze away from Gabe's, she frantically mopped at the spreading red stain with her napkin.

He reached across the table and grasped her hand, his thumb circling her palm. "Leave it. We need to settle this now. Why do you mistrust me, Sarah? How can I possibly help Mike when you act like I'm Jack the Ripper?"

A surge of male heat and the faint essence of his tangy after-shave stole what breath she had managed to salvage. Wave after wave of desire broke over her, causing her to fight as never before against her own needs. Life wasn't about desire. Life was about practicality, commitment, responsibility. She *had* to end this. "Perhaps you seduced the last mother you dealt with in the program, but *I* didn't sign my son up because I was a sex-starved divorcee."

"Don't be insulting!" he snapped. "The guardian of my former agency assignment was a grandmother. She had warmth and passion enough to take on raising her wayward son's child—to keep the boy from living in drug-infested squalor. That, Sarah, is what breeds respect."

Gabe threw down his napkin and got to his feet. "I'm sorry if I stepped over some invisible line. I can be as distant as you want me to be. I told you before that you set the rules." His tone was cold. Harsh.

"Mom? Gabe?" Mike came into the room, doing his best to stifle a big yawn. "Is somethin' wrong?" He looked anxious. "Are you guys mad at me?"

Gabe softened instantly. He quickly plucked up the coffeepot and began filling two cups. This was take it or leave it time, he decided. Sarah's choice. He would miss Mike, but the boy wouldn't benefit if the two adults continued to squabble. He was, however, surprised to see his hand shake.

Sarah jumped up and collected the plate she'd kept warm for Mike. "No one's mad at you, honey, but watch those *g*'s, huh? Come and sit at the counter," she said. "I spilled a glass of wine all over the table. That's what happened. Nothing much."

The child obviously felt relieved. He glanced at Gabe. "Good thing it wasn't you that spilled," he said. "Mom has this boring book on manners. She'd read you the whole thing."

Gabe handed Sarah a cup. Their fingers brushed and she jerked her hand back, nearly spilling again.

Gabe couldn't ignore the attraction that surged between them and wondered how honest she was prepared to be.

Sarah averted her gaze.

Feeling both angry and disappointed, he set her cup on the table.

"You gonna read me a story tonight, Gabe?" Mike stopped shoveling spaghetti into his mouth long enough to ask.

Sarah drew a sharp breath. Bedtime was their quiet time together. The look she flashed Gabe said exactly how she felt.

"It's up to your mom, kicker." Gabe shrugged. "It's been a long day. I'll probably leave after I help clean up."

"No need for you to stay," Sarah murmured. "The dishes will keep." She avoided Gabe's eyes and turned to Mike. "Early to bed with you, hon. Don't you remember that we're going to hear Harvey sing in the morning? His quartet's doing a special presentation down at Puck's Alley."

"Aw, Mom, do we gotta?" Mike screwed up his face. "Maybe Gabe needs me to help again at his boat tomorrow."

"A boyfriend?" Gabe asked lightly.

"Yeah," Mike said in a sour voice, "Harvey Denton. He don't like kids."

"Denton?" Gabe snorted.

"You know him?" Mike stopped eating to stare.

Gabe nodded, crossed his ankles and tugged on his earlobe.

"Not that it's any of your business," Sarah interjected primly, "but he's a colleague. I work for Lou Page."

"Lou's a nice man," Gabe said. "Denton's a jackass."

"Is that like stuffy?" Mike asked curiously. "Don'cha 'member? I said today how I didn't like Mom's friend, Harvey."

"You discussed me?" Sarah was indignant.

Gabe held up a hand. "It wasn't like it sounds. And this argument is going nowhere. Kicker, tomorrow you spend the day with your mom. I'll see you Wednesday at practice."

He deposited his cup on the counter and gave Mike's arm a light punch. "Sarah, you have my business card," he said. "If you want to settle where this goes from here, call me. For now, I'll say good-night."

His departure was so sudden Sarah was left feeling as if some vital force had gone with him. She went through the motions of stacking dishes and listening to Mike chatter about his great day with Gabe. Long after she had him tucked into bed, she lay awake, vacillating. Perhaps if she let Mike do a few things with Gabe, he'd be more receptive to spending time with Harvey.

After all, Gabe had done nothing wrong. He didn't let Mike get away with bad manners, either. The problem was hers, she admitted after some soul-searching.

She was an adult; she could deal with a small case of lust. She had her friends and Mike had his—which now included Gabe. The two of them, she and Gabe, didn't need to mix socially. From now on, there would be no more cozy little family dinners.

Then why, when it all sounded so logical, did she feel so unsure? Why wasn't her heart convinced? She lay in bed contemplating the shadows of swaying palms that swirled in a ghostly dance across her ceiling until they blurred and faded into daylight.

Sunday arrived before she was ready. Sarah was upset to realize that Gabe held such power over her waking thoughts—and, worse, that he so easily stole her revitalizing hours of sleep. The way she felt now, she'd like nothing better than to call Harvey and beg off.

To keep from acting on that temptation, she assumed a cheerful demeanor and went to awaken Mike. She had to go through with today, if for no other reason than to forget the way her body betrayed her every time she so much as thought of Gabriel Parker.

CHAPTER FIVE

BY SUNDAY EVENING, Sarah wished the day had never happened. She leaned heavily against the kitchen counter and despondently sipped a cup of tea. She'd made it strong but apparently not strong enough to wipe out memories of a day that had started out badly and gotten worse.

She should have had a clue when she'd managed to wake Mike only after threatening to douse him with cold water. Never a morning person, he'd started out grumpier than usual. She'd known, of course, that he didn't want to go anywhere with Harvey. Sarah groaned and let the steam from her tea loosen her tight facial muscles. If only she could blot out the hours after the concert.

Harvey, always scrupulously prompt, nagged from the outset about Mike's attitude. By the time the three of them arrived at Puck's Alley, Harvey was livid, Mike stubbornly sullen, and Sarah, trapped in the middle, was unsuccessfully trying to placate them both.

The more Mike fidgeted, the more Harvey scowled at him, and the more forced Sarah's smile became.

She took a long swallow of the hot sweet tea and sighed. If only she'd insisted Harvey drive them straight home after the performance. But no, she'd let herself be talked into brunch at the stately old Royal Hawaiian Hotel. Had she really believed luxurious beachfront dining would appeal to a boy who'd been out of sorts since missing hamburgers with his idol?

She groaned again. Apparently she had. And considering everything, Mike really tried. But nothing he did met with Harvey's approval—from squirming too much to being too messy and noisy. And all of that happened *before* the poor kid spotted some surfers out the window and accidentally spilled a full glass of milk on the pink linen tablecloth. The way Harvey carried on, anyone would think Mike had done it on purpose. Not that she was thrilled about his excitement over the surfers, but she defended him because accidents happened and Harvey's reaction was out of line.

In retrospect, Sarah began to doubt that Harvey Denton could ever relate to children. Although she tried hard not to compare him with Gabe Parker, it was evident Harvey would never measure up in Mike's eyes. And after today, he'd slipped in hers too. A lot.

Her teacup hit the saucer with a whack and she grabbed a paper towel to mop up the spill. The final truth had dawned with Harvey's old-fashioned perfunctory kiss at the door. He had delivered the quick peck on her lips as usual and she realized what had been missing all along—the zing she'd experienced last night with no more than a simple touch from Gabe Parker.

Horrified she could develop such feelings for another surfer, Sarah clung to the sink to keep her knees steady. She felt suddenly drained, exhausted, and emptied her tea down the sink. Then she snapped off the light, welcoming the velvety darkness. She dared the preposterous thought to surface again. Relieved to see it fade, she started for bed, stopping to check on Mike.

He was asleep, snoring softly. One wiry arm was thrown across his ratty old bear. Sarah tiptoed out, closing the door quietly behind her. To her knowledge, he hadn't needed Bear-Bear since Gabe had come into his life. If that wasn't a testament to Mike's bad day, she didn't know what was.

In her own room, Sarah eased out of her dress and into a nightshirt. During the routine of brushing her teeth and washing her face, she paused to study the shadows around her eyes. She wished there was a Bear-Bear to offer her some comforts, too. Because in spite of what her parenting books claimed, she couldn't help thinking everything was her fault.

Farrell's leaving. Harvey's disapproval. The complications Gabe Parker presented. Each came about as a direct result of her actions.

Tears suddenly pressed for release. Sarah struggled to hold them in, but they slipped out, anyway, when she climbed into bed, soaking her pillow. Hours passed before she slept.

Monday morning came too fast. Fortunately the normal hustle and bustle kept her from dwelling on the weekend. Unfortunately, she was running late—as usual. On the positive side, though, Mike was so busy searching for lost sneakers, he didn't notice her unhappiness.

As this wasn't his Monday for going to school early, Sarah had to drop him off at Mitzi's mother's. When they arrived at the Shinns', one shoe was still untied, he had a half-eaten piece of toast in one hand and the revered soccer shoes in the other.

Either the shoes no longer presented an issue or she was too tired to care. Whichever, this morning the sight of them didn't even spark a reaction. Nothing. Hallelujah!

"Mike," she yelled after him. "Remember to call me at work if Coach is going to bring you home. If he is, I may work late."

"Aw, Mom," grumbled Mike, his words muffled by the last bite of toast as he knelt on the walkway and dealt with his untied shoe. "Jim Cline only has to call his mom if Coach *isn't* taking us home. Why can't I do that? You make me call for every little thing."

Sarah dredged up a smile. She remembered Mitzi's comment about letting go. "Uh . . . sure, hon. We'll give it a try. Just call if you need me to pick you up. Otherwise, I'll expect you home by six."

"Really?" He grinned. "All right!" he hollered, loping off toward Mrs. Shinn's front door, his shoestring loose again.

Such a small thing to make him so happy. If only that was all it took for her, she reflected as she drove to Mitzi's. Uh-oh. Mitzi was pacing at the curb, and she looked decidedly annoyed.

"You're half an hour late again, Sarah. How you can get behind on Monday morning is always a mystery to me. I swear, one of these days I'm going to sleep an extra fifteen minutes."

Sarah laughed. "You do, and it'll be the one morning I'm early. But I thought Sam was due back. So how come *you're* on time? Didn't you fix him breakfast?"

"Breakfast? On his first morning back? Sarah, I'm afraid you've been without a man too long." Mitzi fastened her seat belt, then stretched like a contented cat. "We didn't start the day with breakfast—but it was delicious all the same."

"Mitzi!" Sarah blushed.

Dark eyes gleamed wickedly. "Come on, Sarah. Women are allowed to enjoy sex, too. Don't you remember?"

Sarah rounded the corner a little too fast and was forced to brake. "Can't say I do," she said dryly. "If I ever felt that way it's been so long I've forgotten." Except that wasn't true. All too vividly she recalled the rush of desire she'd experienced Saturday night. And Gabe Parker hadn't even *kissed* her, for mercy's sake. Her ears began to burn.

Mitzi braced an arm against the dash. "I hope you don't think I discuss my sex life with everyone. You're my best friend. You see how miserable I am when Osamu's gone. Honestly, Sarah, I don't know how you cope alone."

"I'm not exactly alone," Sarah pointed out. "I have Mike." Although that was hardly what her friend meant.... Abruptly she changed the subject. "This was Sam's last out-of-town match for a while, wasn't it?"

"He has three more this year. But the good news is he'll be home for the Maxwells' party. Last night he suggested I buy a sinfully extravagant dress. If you're going, why don't we give you a ride to the party?"

Sarah pretended to be preoccupied. Mitzi repeated the offer.

"I—I haven't decided," Sarah said. "Lou arranged for me to go with Harvey, but he and I had a...little falling-out yesterday."

"Harvey." Mitzi snorted. "He'd leave you sitting alone while he conducted business. You need to let go a little. Dance. Have fun. I wish we knew some nice unattached man."

"I've almost decided to stay home. It's really a couples thing."

"Nonsense. Maybe you'll meet someone there. Get a sexy new dress. It'll be fun. The three of us will kick back and hang loose."

Sarah coasted up to the curb and parked in the shade of a fat banana palm. She sighed heavily. "Sometimes I think Sarah Michaels can't hang loose, Mitzi. There are times I wonder if I lived under my father's military regimen for so long I can't relax."

Mitzi's gaze narrowed. "The Sarah Michaels I know can do anything she sets her mind to. Now hear this. We *are* going on a shopping spree. Let's say next week, one day after work. I'll ask Mom to keep Mike. Now, don't object. I won't take no for an answer." She leapt from the car.

Sarah shook her head as Mitzi departed. She watched her skip up the walkway and wondered when, if ever, *she'd* had that much energy. Yet it was impossible to be around Mitzi and not share some of her enthusiasm.

By the time Sarah reached her building she'd begun to refigure her monthly bills, to see how much she could squeeze out for a dress. It might be just what she needed to lift her spirits.

Imbued with Mitzi's zest for living, Sarah took the stairs, instead of the elevator. Or was it to avoid Harvey, who had a tendency to blame her tardiness on her son? This morning she didn't feel like dealing with one of his lectures.

Good. His door was closed. Sarah went to her desk. Lou and the other lawyers also appeared too busy to notice her late arrival. She turned on her computer and caught the telephone on the first ring, popping a tape into her transcriber with a free hand. All in all, she found routine comforting, Sarah thought, as she got up to pull a file. Which was why she should never have married a spur-of-the-moment man.

And now Mitzi was suggesting she throw caution to the winds again. The notion amused her, even as she listened to Harvey drone monotonously on the tape. She was working on his final brief when a new client arrived for him. Sarah hit his intercom. As was customary, he came out. What *wasn't* customary was the way he lingered, chatting idly with the petite red-haired woman.

According to her file, the new client was being sued by her deceased husband's children for a greater share of his estate. Privately, Sarah thought her story didn't quite match the shrewdness of her eyes. In fact, Sarah felt sorry for Harvey and wondered why he didn't refer the case to one of the new staff lawyers.

So she was shocked when he came out at noon and instructed her to make reservations for two at an exclusive restaurant on the bay. The woman clung to his arm and he put on a disgusting display of jocularity so totally out of character that Sarah wondered if it had been for her benefit. Was he trying to make her jealous?

The idea was ludicrous. But right then, Sarah knew she'd never truly considered Harvey a love interest. Almost sadly, she mourned the loss of what apparently had never been—the possibility of remarriage some day.

The telephone shrilled. She reached out absentmindedly. "Page and Associates," she said, her voice a little husky with regret.

"No wonder Lou Page is one of the most successful lawyers on the island," drawled a teasing baritone. "I'd switch firms in a minute for a chance to meet a lady with such a sexy voice."

Sarah's heart rate escalated—until she recalled how, on this very telephone, he had flirted with Sheena Maxwell.

Gabe Parker charmed women as naturally as some men breathed.

"What can I do for you?" Sarah employed her most professional tone. "Everyone's at lunch, but I'll be happy to take a message."

He hesitated briefly. "I'm calling you, Sarah. I'm afraid I have to cancel out on Mike's game next week."

Last week, Sarah had been prepared for such a call. Today, having been lulled into complacency by his attentiveness, she lacked a ready reply.

"Sarah?"

"I heard." She paused. "You're giving me plenty of notice. Frankly, that's more than I expected."

"Dammit, Sarah, why do you always make it sound like I'm unreliable? I hate doing this, and I want to tell him myself. The reason I called was to ask if I could pick him up from practice tonight and maybe take him out for the hamburgers I promised. Obviously that's not a good idea. Forget it. Handle telling him however you think is best. Goodbye."

"No. Wait. Gabe—" A sharp click met Sarah's belated protest. She frowned at the buzzing receiver for a moment and drummed her fingers on the desk. She'd been unforgivably rude. And if Mike ever found out she'd denied him a burger with Gabe for omelets at home, well...

Digging in her purse, Sarah found the card Gabe had given her. Considering the hour, she took a wild guess and punched out the numbers to the marina.

"Parker," growled a voice at the other end.

Sarah wasn't sure the phone had even rung. Did that rough voice belong to Gabe or another Parker? "Gabe?" she asked timidly. "Is that you?"

"You expected one of my harem, maybe? Sorry to disappoint you, Sarah. What do you want? I'm too busy today for games."

Sarah chewed her lip. "I don't blame you for being cross. I was rude earlier. I called back to tell you that Mike would be in seventh heaven if he got to go out for hamburgers with you."

The silence stretched for so long Sarah tasted blood on her lip. Well, it was up to him. If he didn't want to accept her apology, that was his problem. When it appeared he wasn't going to, she threw his card into her middle drawer and slammed it closed. She'd just started to hang up and almost missed his soft response.

"My offer stands," he said in a weary voice. "I wonder, though, what's behind your sudden change of heart. Did good old Harvey come back and invite you to choir practice? Or with Mike gone, will you and the choirboy make a little music at home?"

"It's a quartet. And he—that is, we..." She gave a sigh of frustration. "Just forget it, Parker. For your information, Harvey took a classy redhead to lunch today and I haven't seen him since."

"Jealous?" he shot back.

"Certainly not," she told him. "Not that it would be your concern if I was. So, are you or aren't you picking Mike up tonight? I'm busy, too."

"Temper, temper. Look, if you're really not tied up tonight, come with us." He said it lightly, but Sarah didn't want to be tempted. Especially after making the decision to keep their social lives separate. She battled temptation for so long Gabe finally spoke.

Actually he laughed. "I thought as much," he said. "I'll have Mike home early—before you call the cops." He hung up, and Sarah slammed her receiver down. For two cents she'd show up at the parking lot and horn in on their outing. Except that Mike would be embarrassed if she did, and after that lunch with Harvey, he deserved some fun.

Off and on throughout the day, Sarah fantasized about Gabe's reaction if she did show up. She could just picture his shock. In the midst of relishing one such vision, Harvey and his attractive client returned. They were two hours late and Sarah wasn't bothered a bit.

By then she'd made up her mind to forgo working overtime. With Mike busy, if she left on time she could treat herself to a leisurely bubble bath, something she never did during the week. Maybe it wasn't exactly outrageous, but the fact that she was free to indulge such a fancy seemed just a little luxurious.

The moment Sarah picked Mitzi up, her friend noticed something was different. "I can't put my finger on it," Mitzi said, "but you've definitely changed since morning. You look happier. Say, you didn't go shopping on your lunch hour without me, did you?"

Sarah laughed. "Mitzi, who but you equates happiness with shopping? Can't a person feel good for other reasons?"

"You bet," Mitzi said in droll tones. "But it isn't likely you did *that* on your lunch break, either."

"Mitzi, you're terrible. Osamu really should stay home more. Not everyone equates a quick roll in the hay with happiness, either."

"Who said anything about quick?" Mitzi wrinkled her nose and grinned. "So, if not a man, what?"

"If you must know, Gabe called unexpectedly. He's taking Mike out for hamburgers tonight. So I'm going home to soak in the most lavish bubble bath in history. Now, that may not sound exciting to you, but for a single mother with a child who's liable to parade little friends through the house at all hours, it's a slice of heaven."

Mitzi cocked her head. "Gabe Parker is spending a lot of time with Mike. Is that normal?"

"Normal, how?" Sarah's smile slipped. "Surely you don't mean—"

"Of *course* not," Mitzi interrupted. "I just wondered if he's hanging out with Mike because the boy has a gorgeous mother?"

Sarah jerked her car to a stop in front of Mitzi's house. Her furious silence spoke volumes.

"Okay, okay. Forget I said anything." Mitzi wasted no time climbing out. She shut the car door firmly behind her.

Leaning across the seat, Sarah rolled down the passenger window. "Wait, Mitzi. Don't mention anything of the sort to Sam. Not even in jest. If a rumor like that got back to Gabe... I mean, I'm not exactly in his social circle. I wouldn't want him to think I was interested."

Mitzi tossed her famous backward wave and continued into the house.

Sarah sat for a moment, debating whether to follow her—to make her position on the matter absolutely clear. But if she did that, Mitzi would no doubt say she was protesting too much. And she wouldn't have time for her bath.

"Ooh, but that woman can be so maddening," Sarah sputtered, grinding the old car's gears as she let out the clutch too fast. Tomorrow, she'd lay it on the line for her friend once and for all.

At home, it was as if fate conspired against her plans. First, Sarah's absentminded neighbor called her over to complain that she thought someone was stealing Kukui nuts from her trees at night.

If the woman hadn't been dead serious, Sarah would have laughed it off. The polished nuts sold well to tourists, but she'd never heard of anyone stooping to rustle them. More than likely, Mrs. Lawrence had raked them and forgotten. Still, Sarah knew the old woman was often lonely, so she spent an extra few minutes listening.

When she finally broke away and let herself into the house, the phone was ringing. It was Jim Cline's mother wanting to discuss the end-of-season soccer banquet. Sarah thought it was a little early since the season had just started, and she said so. She'd no more than hung up when Mrs. Cline called again about another fund-raiser for the uniforms. Sarah would have forgone her bath in favor of parental duty—if the woman hadn't kept turning the conversation to Gabe Parker.

Sarah thought afterward that she hadn't been altogether nice in her attempt to nip gossip in the bud. But darn! She stalked into her bedroom, shed her clothes and shrugged into a robe. She turned both taps on full and was pouring in her bubble mixture when the telephone rang again.

It had to be that nosy Mrs. Cline calling back. Sarah swore and grabbed up the receiver. "Yes? What is it this time?"

"Hi!" Gabe sounded somewhat mystified. "Sarah? Is that you?"

Sarah flopped down on the bed and snatched up her clock. Had it stopped? "Where are you?" she asked breathlessly. "Is anything wrong? Where's Mike?"

"Whoa. Stop," he said. "Your line's been busy. I wanted you to know Mike and I are at the restaurant. We won't be long. Practice ended early and we didn't want you to worry in case you saw some of his teammates out playing in the neighborhood. Is everything okay with you?"

Sarah had one ear tuned to the rush of water in her tub. Funny, but until this minute, it hadn't even occurred to her that Gabe might not be there to meet her son as he'd promised. She felt a little guilty. "I planned to treat myself to a bubble bath, but it doesn't really matter. I'll let the water out, since you're early."

Gabe's low chuckle sent a tiny prickle of awareness up her spine.

"Need someone to scrub your back?" he teased. "I could be persuaded to give up a hamburger for such a worthy endeavor." She didn't respond and he waited through her tense silence. "Don't go all huffy on me, Sarah. I'm only kidding. We'll give you plenty of time. Happy bathing!"

Sarah sighed as the phone went dead. But she took him at his word and dashed back to wrench off the faucets. Quickly, before anything else could happen, she stripped off her robe and slid in up to her chin. Before long, warm aromatic steam curled soothingly about her head. The day's strain began to ease away.

Sarah tried blanking her mind by identifying all the individual flower scents in her new bubble-bath mixture. Sweet pikake blended smoothly with the pungent spicy scent of plumeria. Her mind drifted.

Idly she pictured herself frolicking in the foaming surf wearing nothing but stacks of leis. Travel posters had a way of making Hawaii's secluded beaches extremely appealing. All at once there was Gabe Parker riding a wave on his bright yellow surfboard and insinuating himself into her private dream. "So much for that," she lamented around a yawn as she settled deeper under the slick scented water.

"Mmm. Nice," she murmured sleepily. Here, in the privacy of her bath, she could be cool and aloof, or tempting as Lorelei. A fantasy Sarah could do things the real Sarah would never do. For instance, she could dance along white sandy beaches and play naked in the surf.

She used her toe to add more hot water. Fantasy was wonderful. Why, it allowed her to explore those ropy muscles of Gabe Parker's arms. Let her savor the salt of the sea on his skin. To kiss and be kissed in return. Time slipped away. The water cooled. And Sarah drifted off.

"Mom!"

Her son's sudden shout, the sound of running footsteps and the realization that he was crying, jerked Sarah awake. Panic-stricken, she leapt from the tub and with shaking hands threw on her robe. Why was it so dark? She started for the door, but nearly lost her footing in a puddle of water that had sloshed over the edge of the tub. Somewhere in the back of her cobwebby mind she heard heavier footsteps pounding down the hall.

"Sarah!"

She headed into the hall, groping for the light switch, then collided with someone breathing hard after running full-tilt.

All at once a bright light blinded her. "Gabe?" She tugged the edges of her robe together and blinked. His hand left the light switch, then reached out to steady her. "Mike! I heard him crying. What's wrong?"

"My question exactly." Yet even as Gabe's eyes softened with relief, his arms tightened around her back, and before either of them had time to think, his lips covered hers, driving her panic deeper—then away.

For a moment her heart pounded. Then one by one her bones dissolved until she clung to him helplessly, kissing him back as she had in her dream.

The front door slammed, but it was Mike's shout that broke them apart. He could be heard running down the hall. Sarah stepped into the bathroom, away from Gabe, and stumbled. Eyes wide and not fully comprehending, she grasped her robe tight beneath her chin and dropped down on the edge of the tub.

None too steady himself, Gabe braced an arm against the door casing.

The boy reached them and stopped. "Is she all right? What's wrong? I went back and shut the Porsche lights off like you said. Oh, Gabe, is she gonna live?" Not only was there a quiver in the small voice, but the light dusting of freckles stood out against a pasty white face.

Gabe shook off his sudden unexpected desire and placed a comforting hand on Mike's shoulder. "Everything's fine, son. I'm not sure, but I think your mom fell asleep in the tub." It struck him then how unsteady his own hand was, and his voice was decidedly rough around the edges.

He urged the boy through the doorway to check for himself.

"You okay, Mom? I—I was scared." Mike's voice faltered.

Sarah held out both hands and her son ran to her, flinging his arms around her neck.

"You scared us half to death, Sarah," Gabe said. "The house was dark, so I walked Mike inside. We knew you'd planned a bath, and he ran down the hall to check. I died a thousand times when he tore back, crying that you'd drowned. I sent him outside on an errand and came in myself, not knowing what I'd find."

"But you said I had time for a bath," she said, smoothing a hand over her son's hair.

Gabe arched a brow. "It's two hours since I called, Sarah. I assumed that was time enough. As it was, we blew an extra hour at the Queen Emma Museum."

"The museum?" she squeaked. "No kidding?"

"Yeah, Mom!" Mike exclaimed, pulling back to look at her. "I came to tell you the museum was cool. But the onliest light on was the hall night-light and you didn't hear me." He buried his face in her neck and hugged her again. "You didn't move! I thought you was dead."

"Were," she corrected, although she cradled him close. "I'm so sorry. I'd never scare you on purpose." A shiver swept through her, and her voice caught. "My mother was sick a lot—an invalid. Military duty kept my father away from home. I was always afraid something terrible would happen to Mother when we were alone." She rocked him gently. "I don't ever want you to worry like that. Remember we discussed all this when I showed you pictures of your grandparents?"

Mike sniffed and nodded. "I 'member."

Gabe's heart lurched. And he'd thought *he* was neglected because his father was off building a fortune. Compared to Sarah's life, his had been a regular picnic. His mother doted on him and his brother. If only he'd known some of this before.

"Come on, kicker," he said gently, grasping the boy's shoulders and pulling him away. "How about if I have a look at that radio you said quit working? We'll let your mom get dressed before she takes a chill."

Although he addressed the child, his darkly troubled gaze rested on Sarah a moment before skipping away.

She loosened her grip on her son and drew her robe closer. "I'm fine, really," she assured Mike when he hesitated. "I do need to dress. Why don't you two take the radio into the kitchen where the light's better?"

What exactly was that look in Gabe's eyes? she wondered. Pity? Sorrow? Regret that he'd kissed her? None of those prospects seemed particularly flattering, considering what had just happened between them.

Rather self-conscious now, she stood and urged them toward the door.

Unable to help himself, Gabe let his gaze drift back over her face and the hair she had piled atop her head, now falling loosely about her cheeks.

She glanced up and caught him unawares.

Without thinking, he reached out and ran a finger along her jaw, just to convince himself she really was all right.

"You comin', Gabe?" The boy paused in the hallway, sounding unsure.

"Um, yes." He spun on his heel, adding, "You bet. Let's go take a look at that radio."

A minute ticked by as Sarah imagined she still felt the sensual touch of his fingertips and saw the look in his deep blue eyes. Her pulse climbed.

Letting out the water, she began to reconstruct what must have been a frightening scene. She hurried to dress, deciding that Gabe's kiss had been the understandable result of the moment's tension.

But what, if anything, did his last look mean? Did he find her attractive?

No. That was preposterous. Gabriel Parker moved among the really beautiful people. Like Sheena Maxwell. But Sarah wasn't so naive that she didn't realize he might dally outside his circle if a woman was willing.

Was that how he saw her? Willing? Attempting to brush her hair, she encountered snarls. She threw down her brush. Well, she wasn't. But one good thing had come of this incident. Mike did love her. So Gabe hadn't siphoned off as much as she'd imagined.

Sarah pulled on a pair of clean jeans and a knit top. Was it losing her son's affection to the age-old allure of male bonding that had her running scared? Or was she simply afraid for her own heart?

Somber brown eyes gazed back at her from the mirror. What they suggested was that it might already be too late. She ran a shaking finger over her lips. Maybe she *was* willing. It wouldn't be such an unpleasant experiment finding out. Her step quickened as she went in search of her son—and Gabe.

But Mike was alone in the kitchen, his radio blaring.

"Where's Gabe?" she asked casually, thinking maybe he'd gone to put away his tools.

The boy glanced up, "He left."

"Left?" Sarah heard the disappointment in her own voice.

"Yep." Mike nodded. "Said he hadda go meet Sheena. But don't worry, he 'splained to me about missing my next game."

Sarah's mouth opened and closed. "Explained," she corrected, all the while feeling her short-lived joy shrivel. She should have known. Men like Gabe Parker were masters at explanations and excuses. How could she have allowed herself to be taken in by another no-good charmer?

CHAPTER SIX

ONCE AGAIN, morning came too soon. Sarah stared at her reflection in the mirror and told herself sternly that the sleepless nights had to stop. She was an adult. A mother. Not a love-struck teenager.

Her feelings for Gabe had run temporarily amok, that was all. So he had a date with Sheena. Big deal. The simple kiss she'd shared with him was due to nerves on both sides. The telephone rang as Sarah battled a stubborn little voice insisting that nothing about Gabe's kiss was simple.

"'Lo," she said, snatching up the receiver of her bedside phone. Gabe's warm chuckle drifted across the line when she'd been expecting Mitzi.

"The word, I believe is *hel*lo." He enunciated clearly, correcting her the way she corrected Mike. "So, Sarah, good morning," he said into her silence. Then his slow easy humor vanished and his voice took on an intimate quality. "I couldn't go to work this morning without knowing how you were. I hated leaving last night before you came out. What took you so long?"

His sincerity battered at the walls Sarah had rebuilt around her heart. "I'm fine...really," she said, her tone rivaling his for intimacy.

"That's good. You gave Mike quite a jolt. Me, too," he added after a moment's hesitation. He almost felt her waging some internal battle and didn't want to come on too strong in case he scared her away.

Sarah twisted the telephone cord around her index finger. More barriers tumbled down. "It was good of you to take time from your date to help Mike fix his radio. I'm sure that helped him put the incident from his mind."

There was a silence on Gabe's end, then he said rather gruffly, "I didn't have a date. Sheena's family and mine are good friends, that's all. After her time in France, she's experiencing some difficulty fitting back in with her old crowd. For crying out loud, Sarah, there's ten years difference in our ages."

Sarah's heartbeat accelerated. "I didn't mean to offend you. Mike said..." She frowned, trying to remember what exactly Mike had said. "Well, maybe I assumed it was a date," she offered a bit defensively.

"I'm not a man to go from kissing one woman to a date with another. I know society columnists link me with lots of women, but they're wrong. I do not hop from bed to bed." Now that was dumb, he thought. Would she translate it to mean he only wanted to take her to bed? He waited, holding his breath.

Even in the privacy of her bedroom, Sarah blushed. She had never learned to talk openly about sex. "I...ah...I'm going to be late for work," she ventured at last. Why was he telling her all this? Unless...unless he was interested?

"Don't let me keep you," he said quickly. Lord, he didn't need another misunderstanding with this woman. "Uh...I called to make sure Mike told you I'll pick him up next Tuesday. We'll practice kicks and blocks in the school soccer field."

Sarah's heart slid back into its rightful place in her chest. "No. He didn't say a word." She rubbed her brow. Next Tuesday was the night she and Mitzi were shopping for dresses.

"I'll drop him off afterward, but I can't come in," Gabe continued. "I'm going to Kauai on business and I'll be gone until late Friday. Is there a problem?" At her murmured response, he added, "Did I hear some hesitancy in that no?"

Gabe was observant, Sarah would give him that. Not many men, or at least not the ones she knew, would have picked up on so subtle a nuance. "No, no problem. It's just that Mitzi and I are doing some shopping Tuesday after work. Coach agreed to take him to her mother's around six."

"If you're not going to be too late, I'll stay with him."

"It may be close to eleven."

"Give me the address. I'll take him to the sitter myself."

"It's out of your way," Sarah protested.

"Sarah." He sounded exasperated. "If it's on this side of the island, it's not out of my way. So what are you shopping for? Anything exciting?"

"Not really," Sarah said. "Dresses for the Maxwell party."

"I didn't realize you were going." And what a pleasant surprise it was, too. Just the thought of it made the event more palatable to Gabe.

"We aren't gate-crashing. Mitzi's husband was invited," Sarah said when he fell silent. "I'm only going because Lou insists on it."

Gabe laughed. A deep joyous sound. "You think I get dressed in a penguin suit for a lark? It's business for me, too, Sarah. Only now that I know you're going, the prospect seems brighter."

"Oh...well..." Sarah struggled to breathe. What was he doing?

"Look, I know you're running late. I won't keep you. Give me the address of Mitzi's mother and have a good time shopping next week."

She gave him the information, surprised she remembered it in her current state of confusion.

"Buy something sexy," Gabe growled just before hanging up. He contemplated what would look sexy on Sarah. Just about anything, he decided.

Sarah clung to her receiver, her palms damp.

"Are you ready, Mom?"

She looked up and saw her son. Miracle of miracles, he was dressed and his hair was combed.

"Who called?"

"Gabe," she said, dropping the receiver with some haste.

"Did he say anything 'bout next Tuesday?"

"Yes. Why didn't you tell me what was in the works?"

He shrugged. "'Cause Gabe said he might have a 'pointment. Said he'd call."

"Far—Mike!" Sarah turned and threw up her hands. "Please speak each word slowly and don't leave out any letters. The word is appointment. Honestly, what do your teachers say about your English?"

He looked contrite. "Same as you. But they're all women, too."

"What has that got to do with anything?" Sarah put her hands on her hips.

"Men don't care 'bout things like English. Coach don't preach to me 'bout verbs. Gabe, neither."

"Either," corrected Sarah. "They may not bring it up, but you don't hear them dropping letters or using bad grammar. Next year, we'll request a male teacher for you."

"Oh, no!" Mike rolled his eyes. "Not Mr. Kitzel. He's like Harvey."

Sarah turned and picked up her purse. "There's nothing wrong with Harvey's English."

"Oh, brother," Mike muttered. "Can we go? I'll try to be better, Mom. Don't make me spend more time with Harvey."

Sarah chose to let the remark go. She drove Mike to school without lecturing.

The remainder of the week and the weekend passed in a blur of work and household chores. Only a few times did she wonder what Gabe was up to. Monday he left a message on her machine confirming Tuesday's arrangements. So she wouldn't worry, he told her. How thoughtful of him.

Next morning, Sarah dropped Mike off as usual. He clambered across the seat and gave her a wet kiss. "I hope you get a sexy dress, Mom. 'Course, I think you're real pretty. But if you get something sexy, everybody else'll think so too. 'Bye."

Sarah raised a hand to her cheek. What did eight-and-a-half-year-old boys know about sexy? His parting shot mirrored one Gabe had made last week, and that brought an unexpected blush.

From the moment Sarah stopped for Mitzi, her friend talked nonstop. "Do I ever have good news!" she said by way of greeting. "I talked to one of my cousins last night. He owns a clothing shop in Honolulu. They just got in a new shipment of dressy dresses. I called two other cousins with stores and they're well stocked, too. Can I sniff out bargains or what?"

Sarah smiled. "The man who fixed my air conditioner was your cousin. Do you have relatives in every business in town?"

"Nope." Mitzi laced her fingers in her lap and looked smug. "But where I don't, Osamu does. Don't be smart. Tonight, you're my cousin, too."

Sarah laughed outright. "The black sheep? Which side of the family?"

"Hey, we don't get that specific," Mitzi scoffed. "Let's eat out tonight. We haven't done that in a long time."

Sarah thought about her strained budget. "I probably won't be hungry, Mitzi, but I'll get tea or something." She pulled up to the curb to let Mitzi out and looked away so her friend wouldn't offer to pay. It had taken more than creative financing to find the money for a dress. Just this morning, Sarah had noticed Mike's jeans were getting too short again. Maybe she should skip the party. *And miss seeing Gabe?* a little voice pestered.

"Don't worry about dinner, Sarah," Mitzi said lightly. "You know me—shopping is sustenance enough." Wiggling her fingers, she hopped out and dashed away into her building.

As she parked, Sarah worried again about finances. Before reaching her office, she'd decided to call Mitzi and beg off. There was also the matter of soccer camp. Mike had his heart set on going, and she had more or less agreed.

Since she'd driven Mitzi to work today, Sarah was shocked to find Osamu Kealoha lounging in Lou's doorway when she walked in.

"To what do we owe this honor, Sam?" she teased, "Did one of your students get too aggressive? Or a parent?" It was an old joke and no secret that overenthusiastic parents caused him more problems at wrestling matches than his students.

He laughed, his eyes crinkling at the corners. "Actually I was at the barber's down the street. Mitzi called and said she'd forgotten to pay you for gas this month. Since I was so close, I decided to drop it by."

Sarah straightened from the drawer where she was putting her purse. "No such thing, Sam. She gave it to me in advance—so I could get my air conditioner fixed."

The short muscular man dropped some money on her desk and promptly headed for the door. "Mitzi's never wrong about money. Now, cars are a different story. And since she refuses to take the bus, it's worth twice what you charge just to know she's not wiping out the side of a Mercedes. I love her dearly, but I tell you, put her behind the wheel and she undergoes a personality change." He rolled his eyes. "Look at it this way, you're saving me a lawsuit." Tossing a wave at Lou, he slipped out the door.

Sarah stared down at the fifty dollars.

Lou came to lean on her desk. "While we're on the subject of money," he said, clearing his throat. "I completely forgot your raise. I talked to all the associates a few weeks ago. We agreed your work load has doubled. We're giving you a new title, too. How does legal assistant sound?"

Sarah sank back in her chair. Lou disappeared into his office, then came back with the firm's checkbook. He filled in a generous amount, signed it and ripped the check out.

"I made this retroactive to the first of the year, Sarah. That was when our business really picked up. Forgive my lapse of memory, but I've been so damned busy in court lately." He capped his pen and handed Sarah the check.

She gaped at the figures. Tears welled. "I don't know what to say, Lou." She swallowed and looked away.

"Don't say anything. You earned every penny. By the way, Sam mentioned you and Mitzi are shopping for the Maxwell party. Bring me the bill. I'll reimburse you. After all, I asked you to represent the firm."

"Absolutely not!" Sarah squared her shoulders. "The raise I accept because we *are* busier. You will not buy me a dress out of company funds. Anyway, I'm not sure I'm going."

"I thought it was all set." Lou closed the checkbook and glanced up in surprise. "Isn't Harvey picking you up?"

Sarah caught her bottom lip between her teeth.

Lou scratched his head. "You and Harvey have a tiff? Is that why he's acting like such a moron over the widow Lewis?"

"We didn't really." Sarah flushed. "Well, maybe. Harvey doesn't have much patience with Mike, I'm afraid."

Lou looked thoughtful. "Isn't much point in dating him then, is there?"

Sarah shook her head sadly.

"So how's young Parker getting along with the boy? I haven't heard you mention any problems lately."

Sarah didn't think she wanted to discuss Gabe. "Ah, well, like you said, Lou, you've been in court a lot."

"What kind of answer is that? How does Mike relate to Parker?"

The question made her frown. "They're like two peas in a pod."

"Do I detect a 'but'?" Lou narrowed his gaze. "You know I care about you and the boy. Do I need to throw the bum out on his ear?"

"No." Sarah's laughter spilled over. "Everything's fine between Mike and Gabe. Hey, shouldn't I get at this job you've tagged with a fancy new title?"

"Are you telling me to buzz off, Sarah?" Lou stroked his chin. "I pay you to use that tone with obnoxious clients, not with me. I'm the boss, remember?"

Sarah knew he was teasing. "I do appreciate your concern, Lou. To tell you the truth, I run hot and cold on Gabe Parker myself. With his boat and his surfboard, at first he reminded me of Farrell." Her voice trailed off. "Really, though, they're nothing alike," she said, smiling softly. "Gabe's intuitive. Not at all self-centered. He even makes Mike behave."

Lou tapped his pen on the desk. "So, is the jury is still out?"

Sarah nervously stacked files, recalling her morning conversation with Gabe. "Maybe not," she said quietly. "Maybe it's in."

"A boy needs a full-time father, Sarah."

Sarah looked up sharply. "Not subtle, Lou. You make a better attorney than psychoanalyst."

He chuckled, picked up the checkbook and moved away. "Roger! Say no more. I'll mind my own business—unless you want my advice."

Sarah found his comments disquieting. Was Gabe Parker father material? Throughout much of the day, she caught herself daydreaming about what it would be like being married to him. Unlike Farrell, Gabe was trustworthy. His connection with the sea and the surf didn't seem to be all-consuming, as it was with Farrell and his crowd. He hadn't even mentioned surfing in weeks.

Yet when the more intimate side of marriage stole into her thoughts, Sarah made so many mistakes in her typing she had to put the whole thing from her mind.

By late afternoon, with the burden of finances lifted, she actually looked forward to shopping. At five o'clock, she gathered her things and stopped at Lou's door. "I'm on my way. Thanks again for the raise. You're an angel." She hurried out, knowing he'd bluster and be embarrassed. In her haste she almost bowled Harvey over.

Cloven to his side was Mrs. Lewis. Sarah noticed she'd put aside the black outfit for a frilly pastel dress, one that made her look younger.

"Excuse me," Sarah said, losing no time stepping away from Harvey.

"Sarah. Oh, good." Harvey checked his watch. "I'm glad I caught you before you left." He straightened his tie with a thumb and index finger.

For a moment his eyes drifted to the woman clinging to his arm. Sarah thought he looked guilty about something.

She cocked her head. "I finished typing the Lewis brief. Everything you dictated has been transcribed. It's on your desk. Was there something else you wanted?"

Harvey unbuttoned and rebuttoned his suit jacket. "Sarah, have you ever been properly introduced to Jeanette? I'm certain you've heard of Dane Lewis, the textile king." By way of explanation, he added, "It's his daughter from a previous marriage who's trying to cheat Jeanette out of her rightful share of Dane's estate."

Hadn't she just said she'd typed the whole thing?

Flushing, Harvey went on, "Uh, well, enough of this. It upsets Jeanette." He patted the redhead's hand solicitously. "What I wanted to tell you, Sarah," he said, "is I've asked her to ride with us to the Maxwell party."

Sarah blinked. Hastily blurted statements were not Harvey's normal style.

His hand flew back to adjust the knot in his tie. "It's, ah... Poor Jeanette hasn't been out of her house socially since this whole unpleasantness began. It wouldn't be... good for her to attend a party alone."

Sarah's jaw went slack. She closed her mouth with a snap. "Goodness, Harvey. You don't owe me any explanations. I'm going to the party because it's business. If you like, I can get a ride with Mitzi."

She caught something like relief crossing Jeanette Lewis's exquisitely made-up face.

Harvey straightened. "Don't be silly. Of course I'll pick you up as planned. Nothing's changed except there'll be three of us. As I won't see you before Saturday, I'll tell you now to be ready at eight sharp. Try not to be late this once." Without a further word or even a goodbye, Harvey dragged

Jeanette through the door and left Sarah shaking her head in puzzlement.

Late again, she took the stairs two at a time. She could hardly wait to tell Mitzi about this new development.

"You're kidding!" was Mitzi's reply. "The nerve of that man. Who's he trying to bluff? He's so transparent. Ten to one it's the Lewis millions that interest good old Harvey."

"I don't know about that, Mitzi. He seemed awfully flustered over breaching etiquette by inviting two of us. You know Harvey."

"Well, he did breach it good. You were his date. Why do you stand for that garbage?"

"It wasn't really a date. Lou gave both of us the invitations. For business. Anyway, I never would have told you if I'd known you'd start preaching. I thought you'd get a good laugh. I think it's hilarious." Sarah slowed for a taxi and fell silent as the narrow Honolulu streets thickened with traffic.

Mitzi flopped back in her seat. "It is kind of amusing. Prissy Harvey with two dates. You never know, she may be using him, too. It's okay if she ruffles his immaculate feathers, but promise me, if she gets catty, you'll ride home with us."

"Done," laughed Sarah. "Now that you have my life in order, direct me to your cousins. Or did you want to eat first?"

"Definitely shopping first." Suddenly Mitzi shot her a glance. "You *do* want to have dinner, then?"

"That just slipped out. I intended to let you wonder if Osamu stopped by. Honestly, Mitzi, I love you like a sister, but I won't accept your charity."

Mitzi pulled a face. "I goofed, huh?"

"No. We'll call it your next month's carpooling expense. You might also be interested to know Lou gave me a retroactive raise today."

"Well, it's about time." Mitzi grinned. "Hey, there's my cousin's shop. Park anywhere in the alley."

It seemed to Sarah as if everyone on the island had decided to shop in Honolulu this night. The streets bustled. Her feet ached as she followed Mitzi in and out of stores. Every time she did serious shopping with Mitzi, Sarah swore it would be the last time. Yet here she was again. The woman was relentless, trying on every dress in her size. Sarah was more selective. She looked at dozens. Most were out of her price range even with her raise. Now she studied a frothy number Mitzi begged her to try on. The price jumped out. "We're in the wrong business. I could make this for a quarter of the price if my machine wasn't broken."

"Not me. Have you ever heard about the time I mended the zipper in Sam's pants?"

Sarah returned the dress to the rack. "Don't tell me. He couldn't he get them zipped?"

"He got them zipped okay." Mitzi rolled her eyes. "The problem came later—in a locker room full of students, when he went to dress down for an all-district match. He couldn't get them unzipped."

Sarah laughed.

"Yeah." Mitzi sighed. "Poor Sam. He'll never hear the end of it. It's one of the classic locker-room stories that gets passed down from year to year. He gave my sewing machine to Goodwill."

It was growing dark as Mitzi dragged Sarah into yet another alley and another cousin's store. Now the air was cooler and the streets less busy. Not finding anything there, they moved on to Osamu's list of relatives.

At last in a small shop on a side street, in a section of town that made Sarah slightly nervous, she found a dress she liked—at a good price. Dark jade satin rippled like metallic smoke when she moved. The sides were slit from floor to thigh, allowing a provocative peek at both legs. Sarah slowly revolved in front of the three-way mirror. The material molded gently over her full breasts, yet flowed smoothly over her slim hips and flat stomach. Softly capped sleeves and a high collar closed by satin frogs added richness and lent an air of mystery. And the workmanship was exquisite. Sarah felt like a new woman in it. A princess. If she shopped carefully, she might stretch her dollars to include a pair of shoes. She'd seen the perfect ones in a shop a few streets over. They also had a metallic sheen. Delicate straps with three-inch heels. With them on, her head would touch Gabe's chin.

Piling her hair loosely on her head, Sarah made one last slow pirouette in front of the mirror before deciding. Stray locks fell carelessly about her pale cheeks and her eyes gleamed gold in the dim lighting. Yes, she wanted this dress. It made her look different. Not beautiful, but certainly pretty. And yes, she thought, releasing her pent-up breath in a rush, maybe even sexy.

Mitzi found her dream dress on the same rack. It was midnight blue with a spray of sequined bamboo running from shoulder to knee. The chiffon overlay floated when she walked and added height to her petite frame.

"If I were built like you, Sarah," Mitzi proclaimed, slowly walking around her friend, "I'd buy a dress with a plunging neckline. Still..." She tilted her head. "That one does provoke the imagination."

"Low necklines aren't me, Mitzi. I'm buying this dress," she said decisively. Gabe's face rose before her and caused Sarah a stab to the midsection. Did she really think she could capture his attention at a party abounding with designer dresses? The thought threw a damper on her enthusiasm. "If you've paid for your dress, Mitzi, let's go. This part of town gives me the willies."

"Really, Sarah," Mitzi chided. "This isn't Hotel Street." Her gaze narrowed. "Or do you even know about Hotel Street?"

"I wasn't *that* sheltered. I know it's the street where all the prostitutes are. Servicemen drop a lot of money there when they're on leave."

"Not ordinary prostitutes," Mitzi confided. "Exotic women. Multiethnic. I've heard they're beautiful."

"Does nothing faze you, Mitzi? Prostitution is illegal. I remember my father and other officers working to have the area closed to military personnel. They didn't make it sound exotic. They made it sound sleazy."

"Well, maybe," Mitzi conceded. "But I like the mix of cultures in this area. It's not sleazy. Most people are hard-working folks, trying to make an honest living. And just smell that food. After all our shopping, I'm famished."

Sarah glanced around with some uncertainty. Neon signs touted a variety of restaurants. Most were tucked inside shabby buildings, poorly lit holes-in-the-wall. She tossed her packages into the trunk, then stepped aside for an old man, who wandered close.

"Got a quarter for a cup of coffee, lady?"

She glanced up into a pair of world-weary eyes. Sympathy tugged at her heartstrings. He could be someone's father. She had tucked the five dollars' change from her purchase into her jacket pocket, and she pulled it out now, pressing it into his leathery palm.

He held it up to the light and looked shocked. "Bless you," he mumbled. "You must be a saint."

"Sarah," Mitzi warned. "I didn't mean you should shell out your hard-earned cash to every derelict along the street. Come on. Let's go eat before he passes the word that you're a soft touch."

"But he looked so sad," Sarah maintained, turning her head to watch the old fellow's tottering progress.

Paying her no mind, Mitzi hustled her into a Thai restaurant partway down the block. She selected one of the many empty tables and sat down before she spoke. "He'll probably use the money on wine. Shall I order for us?"

Sarah picked up the menu. "Go ahead. I've never had Thai food. Something smells delicious. Maybe I should have bought him dinner."

"Sarah." Mitzi shook her head. "You should get out more."

After they'd eaten the piping hot spicy dishes that kept appearing like magic, Sarah sat back and rubbed her stomach. "That was wonderful, but terribly filling. I wonder if I can afford shoes after eating so much?"

"That's the best part." Mitzi grinned. "Food here is cheap. You could afford to eat here every night—*and* feed a bum or two." She winked.

"I wonder if Mike would like it," Sarah said suddenly. "He complains that my meals are boring."

"Boring food. That's a new one." Mitzi counted out a generous tip.

"Until the thing with Harvey, I didn't realize I've neglected a whole side of Mike's upbringing. Brunch at the Royal Hawaiian was as foreign to him as Thai food is to me." She lay out her own tip. "Did I tell you how upset Harvey got when Mike spilled his milk?"

Mitzi stood. "Harvey Denton is a horse's patoot. Don't get me started."

"Don't worry, I won't. I want to pick up those shoes. Then I'd better go get my child. He'll probably be asleep. Wow! I didn't realize it was so late. I guess it's a good thing I didn't take Gabe up on his offer to stay with Mike at the house. He would have missed his flight to Kauai."

Mitzi paused at the door. "You didn't tell me Gabe offered. How interesting."

"Don't make a big thing out of it, Mitzi. He felt bad about missing Mike's next soccer game, that's all."

"Sarah, why do you refuse to believe the man might actually like you? He's a normal red-blooded male, isn't he?"

"Oh, yes." Then, because Mitzi raised both eyebrows, Sarah realized how her remark must have sounded. She gave a nervous laugh.

Before they reached the car, Mitzi pounced. "Tell me. He *is* interested, isn't he? Gabe Parker kissed you, didn't he?"

Sarah unlocked Mitzi's side. "Kind of," she muttered, rounding the car.

"Hey, lady. Got a quarter?" A young boy emerged from the darkness and stepped so close Sarah couldn't get her car door open.

"I...I don't have any change," she said, surprised and saddened to see a boy only a few years older than Mike on the streets. So steeped in sympathy was she Sarah missed the flash of the youth's knife.

"So gimme the whole purse. I'm not fussy." The boyish grin was replaced by a look of menace.

Sarah thrust out her jaw. "'Gimme' is not a word," she said as though correcting Mike. "And I will not give you anything. I work hard for my money. You should be ashamed."

Mitzi leapt from the car, her face ashen. "Sarah," she pleaded. "What on earth do you think you're doing?"

"Yeah, what are you?" the boy jeered. "Some goody-goody teacher?"

"I'm a mother," Sarah answered. "I'm going home to my son, and you should go home to your mother."

The boy ripped the purse from her grasp. "You're real loony-tunes."

"Hey!" An angry voice shouted from a darkened doorway. "Leave the lady be, punk. She's a friend." It was the man Sarah had given money to earlier.

The boy ran, but the old man, surprisingly light on his feet, overtook him. With little more than a brief struggle, he returned with Sarah's purse.

"Th-thank you," she stammered. "Here, let me give you a reward."

"Nope. You go home. Take care of that boy of yours. I got a grandson...someplace." Sketching a salute, he melted into the alley.

"A grandson. Where does he live?" Sarah called.

Mitzi grabbed her arm hard and pushed her toward the Mustang. "Let's get out of here, Sarah."

Sarah found that her hands were shaking so hard she had to try three times to get the car into gear. She didn't give the coveted shoes another thought. All the way home, she worried about the nice old man and his nameless grandson.

Mitzi, too, fell strangely silent. When they stopped in her driveway, she sighed. "That was awful. I wish Sam had been there. It makes me mad though, too. Honolulu is my city. I was born here. It used to be safe."

The reality of the incident finally sank in. Sarah shuddered. "If that old man hadn't come back when he did..." She didn't finish her sentence.

"Gives you good reason to cultivate a relationship with Gabe Parker."

"Mitzi. I was almost robbed. Could have been killed."

"Don't tell me. I saw. Whatever made you think you could reason with a mugger even if he was just a kid? You need a husband. You shouldn't be out alone."

"All kids have mothers," Sarah said stubbornly.

"Gadzooks. You *are* loony-tunes. I doubt Gabe will find your bravery commendable. I'm certain Osamu won't."

"Don't tell him, please." Sarah got out to retrieve Mitzi's packages. "I wouldn't want Mike to hear about this. What if something had happened to me?"

"Yeah. What if?" Mitzi pursed her lips as she waited for Sarah to open the trunk. "I don't keep things from my husband. I believe in honesty in marriage. Listen to me, Sarah. You should tell Gabe."

"I think you're reading a lot into one kiss and a few hugs." Sarah slammed the lid of her trunk in exasperation.

"Hugs, too?" Mitzi paused on the sidewalk. "This gets better and better. Tomorrow we're having a serious talk. Now, I'm going in. I'm glad Sam is waiting."

Sarah watched Mitzi glide away and glanced nervously over her shoulder. She crawled back inside the car to wait until she saw Osamu meet Mitzi at the door.

Mitzi's parting comment made her think as she headed for Mrs. Shinn's to pick up Mike. Her thoughts weren't happy ones. What if she didn't arrive home some night? Any court would hand over an eight-year-old boy to his father without qualm. Maybe she *would* tell Gabe—just to get his reaction.

THE FOLLOWING DAY, Mitzi was sick. And the next, Sarah was again spared the threatened heart-to-heart, because her friend had an early-morning eye appointment. Nor did Sarah have to listen at five. Osamu had invited guests for dinner and picked his wife up from work.

Sarah had little enthusiasm for attending Mike's soccer game that evening. By lunchtime she was really in the dumps, and she drove into Honolulu to purchase the shoes to go with her dress. In daylight the streets were much less frightening. But she was in that kind of mood. No underage thug was going to steal her independence. Sarah banished all thoughts of what Mitzi—and Gabe—might have said about such defiance.

The moment she arrived at the soccer field after work, Mrs. Cline asked where Gabe was.

"I'm not his keeper," Sarah snapped rudely.

The woman frowned. "My husband is on the soccer board. He wants to ask Gabe if he'll be our assistant coach. Ned Wilson quit."

Shocked, Sarah hoped they hadn't mentioned such a proposal to Mike. He'd badger Gabe to accept. "That might not be a good idea, Mrs. Cline," Sarah said. "Gabe is...well, he..." She chewed at her lower lip and studied her toes. She hadn't told anyone here that Gabe was merely a volunteer with Befriend an Island Child. She was afraid boys like Jim Cline would tease Mike. "He's very busy with work," she ended lamely.

"So is my husband," Mrs. Cline said. "He happens to think his son is worth the extra effort."

"Mike is not Gabe's son," Sarah said tightly.

She made her way to the far end of the bleachers, more depressed than before. Was that what bothered her? Did she want Gabe to be more?

Mike saw her and waved.

She waved back. He looked so grown-up. Gabe had a hand in his new maturity; Sarah recognized that. And whether she wanted to admit it or not, she missed seeing those two blond heads huddled together. Funny, but she'd never pictured Farrell at one of their son's games. Nor Harvey, for that matter.

Fortunately she had no more time to dwell on the subject. Coach followed through on his promise to start Mike. Sarah watched the boy's confident stance at the toss of the coin. Yes, Gabe deserved credit.

The whole team played well. Sarah threw herself into the spirit of the game and yelled until she was hoarse. At the end of the last quarter the score was even. She chewed her thumbnail and gauged the opposition. In the last few moments of the game, Jim Cline kicked a winning goal. Everyone stood up and cheered for the team's first victory of the season.

Sarah felt a vague disappointment that Gabe had had to miss it.

Jim's father was quite puffed up. He offered to buy pizza for all the players. Although Sarah didn't look forward to hearing Mr. Cline brag about Jim all evening, she wanted Mike to bask in the glory of winning with his teammates.

If only they hadn't gone to Arnold's Pizzeria. All she could think about was the night she'd been squashed in the booth next to Gabe and Sheena. However, Gabe had said the young woman was just a family friend, and she believed him.

That was what was so appealing about Gabe. After Farrell's many deceits, it was nice to find a truthful man.

When they finally climbed back into the car for the ride home, Mike, his face smudged with tomato sauce, stifled a big yawn and said, "I wish Gabe had been there tonight, Mom. He woulda been proud of me. I played the best ever."

"You surely did. I'm proud of you. You can tell Gabe on Saturday."

"But he asked me to call him on Kauai," Mike said as they pulled into the drive and he gathered his beloved soccer shoes and his jacket. "I got his phone number in my room. Can I call now, Mom?"

Sarah's breath caught in her throat. Maybe when Mike was finished relaying his good news, Gabe would ask to speak with her. If so, she'd tell him she'd found a dress....

"How about if you call Gabe after your bath?" Sarah negotiated, thinking the prospect would hurry Mike along.

"Gabe won't care if I'm dirty. 'Sides, he can't see me over the phone."

"I can see you, young man, and I want you clean. And you promised me you'd take more care with your English. The word you slaughtered is *be*sides."

Sarah heard her son still muttering as he turned on the bathtub faucets. She grimaced to herself and slowly followed Mike into the bathroom, picking up the trail of clothing he'd left strewn in his wake.

"Gabe would care about a lot of things if he had to live with you," she told him. "That I promise." She shook his dirty clothes under his nose before depositing them in the hamper.

Mike giggled. "I'll bet he wouldn't. I'll ask him and see."

"Don't... don't you dare," Sarah sputtered.

"Why not?"

She was flustered. "Wh-why not?" She took a breath. "Because I said." Then she escaped, her face hot. She'd have to set Mike straight about how two adults generally came to share living quarters.

When the boy reappeared, he'd apparently forgotten their previous conversation. "I'm ready to tell Gabe we won, Mom." He hugged her.

"Do you have his number?"

He held it out. "It's got a lot of numbers. Will you dial?"

"All right." Smiling, she ruffled his clean hair as she punched in the series of numbers. Her heart felt as light and fluffy as a cloud—until the sultry purr of Sheena Maxwell drifted over the wire.

"Parker's suite."

Stunned, Sarah gripped the receiver with both hands to keep from dropping it. Pain, swift and sharp, mingled with anger. Gabe had said this was a business trip. He'd said Sheena was only a family friend. He'd lied, and the betrayal hurt.

She heard Gabe in the background, asking, "Is that Mike on the phone?"

Tight-lipped, Sarah handed the phone to her son. Tears were already sliding down her cheeks as she hurried to her bedroom.

CHAPTER SEVEN

REVENGE! At that moment Sarah wanted to punish Gabe for his cavalier treatment of her feelings. When the tears had stopped, she washed her face and tucked Mike into bed as if nothing was wrong. No easy feat, considering Mike was full of *Gabe saids*.

However, once her maternal duties were finished, she sought refuge in her room. Thoughts of revenge again popped into her head. She pictured herself ordering the most expensive champagne at dear Sheena's party, then dumping it in Gabe's lap. Better yet, she imagined painting hot-pink flowers, the color of Sheena's swimsuit, all over his blue Porsche. Envisioning his response helped salve her shredded ego.

By morning her anger had burned itself out.

By Friday she half expected Gabe to call. All evening she let her answering machine pick up. He called Saturday afternoon, instead. It was her good fortune to have her head under the faucet. Mike answered. Sarah fumed when Mike relayed Gabe's message—that he couldn't wait to see her at the Maxwells' gala event tonight. He had nerve, Sarah gave him that.

Refreshed by a cool shower, she dressed for the party with care. But somehow she lacked the excitement with which she'd shopped for the dress. More than once it crossed her mind to plead a headache and stay home. It wouldn't be untrue, either. A blinding one had settled behind her eyes. But hiding wasn't her style any more than revenge was. Regardless of how it hurt, she would go. For Lou. For the law firm. Everything else had just been the stuff of dreams.

At seven-forty-five, her sitter was late and Harvey was early. Did she have some black cloud hanging over her head, or what?

Harvey paced her living room like a caged bear. "Sarah, it's beyond me how can you be so efficient at work and have your personal life in such shambles."

She dropped a jade earring—one of the few good pieces of jewelry she owned. It rolled beneath a heavy recliner and she paused expectantly, thinking Harvey would offer to retrieve it.

He continued to stand at the mirror, brushing imaginary lint from his jacket. So much for that assumption, Sarah thought. If she wanted to wear jade tonight, it was clear she'd have to recover it herself.

She shoved the bulky chair a few inches, puffed a bit and prayed she wouldn't split the green dress in places other than those designed. Especially when she had to get down on hands and knees. Moments later, out of breath but triumphant, she scrambled up and pushed the chair back where it belonged.

Glancing away from the mirror, Harvey eyed first the chair, then her glowing face and said critically, "Sarah, you pick the damnedest times to rearrange furniture. Go call that sitter. See what's keeping her."

Sarah's cheeks, already warmed by her exertions, blazed. Nor did it help calm her to see Harvey glare at her son, who burst, sweaty and rumpled, through the door with his dirty soccer ball. "Maybe you'd like to pick up Jeanette Lewis and come back for me," she told him, never dreaming he'd do it.

"Good idea." He stepped cautiously around the child so as not to touch or be touched. "Do try to have your domestic problems ironed out by the time we return, Sarah. You know I don't like being late."

"Domestic problems," sputtered Sarah, placing her hands on her hips. "For a nickel, I'd..." But she found herself fuming at a closed door.

"Wow!" Mike sank into the recliner. "If I was older, I'd take you to that old party. You don't look like nobody's mother."

Sarah smiled at her son. "Why, thank you." She giggled, forgetting to correct his grammar. "I'm sure by the time you reach driving age, Mike, you won't be escorting your mother around. Hey, are you okay?" She thought his face looked drawn. Pale. Sarah crossed over and felt his forehead.

He scowled. "Don't like Harvey." He shook off her hand. "Jimmy Cline and me bumped big-time in soccer practice today. Hey, I betcha Gabe'd take you. Why don't I call and ask?" He got up with some difficulty and started toward the phone.

"No, you don't, young man." Sarah caught him by his arm.

He clutched his side protectively. "Why not?"

It would be a tempting idea if it was anyone but Gabe. This was not the night to discuss things with Mike, though. She reached for his shirt. "Gabe has other obligations, for one thing. Stop, let me look. What did you do?"

"There's nothin' to see." He tugged his shirt out of her hands.

She frowned. "Well, I didn't see a bruise. Why don't you call Jenny Sue and see what's keeping her?"

"I know Gabe'd drive you," Mike argued. "When he called earlier, he was surprised you was goin' with Harvey. He thought it was with Aunt Mitzi."

Sarah's breath stalled. The child must be mistaken. Why should Gabe care how she got there? Almost at once the doorbell pealed, and Jenny Sue Jones, the teenager who lived two houses down, burst through the door exclaiming, "Sorry I'm late, Mrs. Michaels." She tossed an armload of school books on the couch, then glanced at Sarah and stopped to stare. "Mrs. Michaels! You look cool!" She gave a thumbs-up.

"Er, thanks, Jenny Sue." Sarah nervously smoothed the clinging material over her hips. She'd never been good with compliments. "Let's talk about tonight's rules, shall we?"

"I know the rules," Mike cut in. "I'm not a little kid no more."

"I've no doubt you know them," Sarah said. "You're also good at bending them." She went on to tick off dos and don'ts, ending by asking again if he was certain he felt all right.

"I'm okay. Kinda pooped is all."

By the time Harvey returned, Mike had stopped bartering for an additional hour of television. He and Jenny Sue were working a Batman puzzle.

Harvey didn't come inside but waited stiffly at the door while Sarah gathered a lacy shawl. She had just stepped outside when she remembered she hadn't given Jenny Sue a number for the hotel. Back she went to look it up.

Harvey protested, "Surely, Sarah, you can't mean you'd actually allow them to call and disrupt your evening?"

"For emergency purposes, Harvey." Sarah barely managed to control her temper.

"How would you get home?" he asked.

He was a pompous ass. Sarah almost laughed. "Don't worry, Harvey, I'd get a cab." She kissed Mike and told him to take it easy.

Harvey made impatient noises. Sarah broke off and handed Jenny money to order in pizza. She slammed the door hard as the man headed down the front steps.

At the bang, he glanced back and flushed, then returned to offer her his arm. "I'm afraid you'll have to sit in the back, Sarah," he said as they neared the car. "Jeanette's dress is quite full. It took five minutes to settle her. It'd be a shame to crush such pretty fabric."

Sarah clamped down on a retort. She could have said it took a full skirt to cover Jeanette's plump backside, but she wasn't given to cattiness. Harvey knew *her* dress was new, too, yet he hadn't made any comment. And he let her climb into the cramped back seat without help. Sarah reminded herself that she was a lady. It struck her then that for all his fancy manners Harvey was no gentleman. She kept silent, thinking it was sad when respect died. Sadder to think what a poor judge of character she'd been.

Jeanette darted a sympathetic glance her way, then began talking nonstop about her case. Harvey could have included Sarah, but didn't. She felt ignored. Insignificant. And by the time they reached the hotel, flat out furious. This wasn't sour grapes, either. No one enjoyed being treated like excess baggage.

She vowed to take that cab home. If she hadn't needed a hand getting out of the car, she'd be history now. Not wanting to make a scene, she went along when Harvey took each woman by an elbow and ushered them both inside.

As always, the Maxwell Reef was the ultimate in elegance and luxury. Tonight, the family had spared no expense in decorating the main ballroom. The entire west wall opened out onto a flagstone patio glowing with Chinese lanterns. Round tables for two, four, six or eight were draped with snow-white linens. Long rectangular tables groaned with hors d'oeuvres. On the patio, tiki torches lit the gently breaking surf. A romantic setting if ever Sarah saw one.

She tried pulling from Harvey's grasp to wander among the baskets of deeply colored island flowers stationed around the room's perimeter. His grip tightened. Before long, in the press of the crowd, Sarah felt smothered by the overpowering perfumes worn by Hawaii's elite.

Harvey stopped to greet two men in formal attire, and she murmured an excuse, intending to slip away. Their conversation ended and he propelled both women to a secluded table. Sarah wasn't pleased, but she had to admit there were no singles being seated. A major drawback to attending formal functions alone, she mused.

Harvey and Jeanette had their heads together. To keep from feeling like a fifth wheel, Sarah studied the battery of white-gloved waiters skittering like so many mice across parquet floors—floors polished to gleam like glass beneath the fragmented light falling from crystal chandeliers. Some waiters carried large trays of hors d'oeuvres, others trays loaded with colorful drinks. In keeping with island tradition, log drums began to throb along the beach, and girls with skin the color of café au lait shimmied effortlessly in time to the demanding music.

As the drumbeats escalated, so did Sarah's pulse. Soon the festive spirit edged out her anger, and she settled back to enjoy the party. After all, this might be her only opportunity to attend such a lavish event.

A passing waiter paused with an array of drinks. Sarah was about to ask which was plain fruit juice when she saw Jeanette watching. She'd be darned if she'd show her inexperience. With panache, she selected a dark red fruity-looking punch in a glass nearly filled with shaved ice. The waiter called it a Scarlett O'Hara.

Sarah smiled. What a fitting name to match her mood. It was tasty, too. Smooth. Cooling to her parched throat. She might have thought differently had she known it contained six parts bourbon to two parts lime juice and a splash of grenadine.

The next waiter to pass picked up Sarah's partially empty glass and promptly left a full one. Except this one was some sort of punch topped with citrus and a tiny umbrella. Sarah nibbled on the citrus as a conventional band replaced the island dancers and Jeanette began to tap her foot against the table leg in an irritating manner. Under her breath, Sarah muttered, "Frankly my dear, I don't give a damn."

Layman Maxwell arrived in a flurry of activity. Sarah stirred the ice in her punch and watched. He looked every inch the millionaire tonight. Mrs. Maxwell was a surprise. Take away the diamonds and she'd be almost dowdy.

All at once Sarah caught sight of Sheena Maxwell, and a piece of ice lodged in Sarah's throat. She choked and Harvey thumped her on the back. "Dowdy" definitely did not describe the birthday girl. Sheena's sleek black creation, slashed almost to her navel, left nothing of her budding maturity to the imagination.

Totally in awe of the young woman's nerve, Sarah took a big gulp of her punch. Then she wished she hadn't, for over the rim of the glass, she saw Gabe Parker. Goodness, he looked splendid in a black tuxedo. The tucked-front white shirt only amplified his deep tan. His honey-blond hair had been neatly trimmed since she'd last seen him. Not trimmed so short, however, that he lost the reckless, swashbuckling air Sarah found maddeningly attractive.

Unable to tear her gaze away, she barely acknowledged Harvey when he suggested she mingle. He and Jeanette were going to dance, he said.

"Mingle?" Sarah watched him leave. It was an unappealing edict. Her limbs felt weighted. Impossible, she knew as Gabe spun the lovely Sheena onto the dance floor.

A waiter snapped up the glass and left a full one. Sarah frowned at the ruby-red liquid. Had she finished that last one? She couldn't remember.

"Don't you look like a beautiful wallflower?" Mitzi's lilting voice jarred Sarah from her intent study of the punch. "Where's old Harv?"

"Out there somewhere dancing with Jeanette Lewis."

"So let's send Osamu to break his legs," Mitzi said lightly. "He has some nerve, leaving you."

"I knew I shouldn't have come, Mitzi. I'm supposed to be here for business reasons, but—"

Mitzi cut off her explanations. "If anyone needs this outing, Sarah, you do." She waved at someone in the crowd. "Oh good, here comes Sam. He stopped to check my wrap." She stood. "It's just too bad if Harvey can't remember who his date is. You come and sit with us."

Sarah let herself be led across the room. "Oh, wait, I left my punch!" she exclaimed.

Mitzi forged ahead. "Leave it," she instructed, and selected just the right table to suit her. "Go have fun. Dance with Sam."

"Will you quit fussing? *You* dance with your husband."

"Thank you, Sarah." Osamu grinned and waltzed his wife into the crowd of dancers. Left to her own devices,

Sarah tapped her foot and hummed. It was warmer over here. She really should have brought her icy punch.

A waiter she hadn't seen before stopped. There were no red drinks on his tray. "Is this lime juice?" she asked, choosing a tall green one.

The man shrugged. "Beats me. I just serve 'em."

One sip of the sour drink and Sarah pushed it aside. The green complemented her dress, but the red tasted better. The notion of color-coordinated drinks made her laugh.

Someone slipped into the chair beside her.

"May I have this dance, gorgeous?" a deep voice said in her ear.

Sarah froze, then whirled so fast her head spun. For a moment, she had difficulty focusing on Gabe's twinkling blue eyes.

"Slumming, Mr. Parker?" Her voice held an edge. "Your volunteer work is with my son, not me."

That stopped him for a minute. Then Gabe stood and hauled Sarah to her feet. "I've done my duty dance for the evening. The rest are for my pleasure." Smiling, he circled her with his arms and twirled her away.

What did he mean by that remark? Sarah wished she didn't have to concentrate to keep from slipping on the shiny floor.

"Relax," he instructed. "Put your arms around my waist and go with the sound. I'm not going to bite, you know. Well, maybe a little nibble," he admitted, laughing as he bent his head and nipped at her ear.

Sarah's steps wavered. Never very proficient at dancing, she landed hard on his toe. Feeling the floor tilt, she grasped his waist, burying her nose in his chest.

"Ah, yes. That's it." He smiled and pulled her against him from shoulder to thigh. "Hang loose. Let me lead." Lord, but she looked like a million bucks tonight. She felt even better. Dare he tell her? She seemed preoccupied. He wished he knew why. He tightened his hold and smiled down at her. Damn, it was good to be back.

Her fingers flexed nervously beneath Gabe's jacket. A big mistake, considering the way his body heat radiated through the thin silk shirt. Feeling her palms grow damp, Sarah slid them restlessly up his back.

A sigh, more like a groan, escaped Gabe's lips. He let both hands skim over the cool satin covering her back. "Did I ever tell you satin makes me crazy?"

She shook her head. A wall seemed to tilt toward her and she ducked.

Gabe pulled her closer and whispered in her ear. "Your perfume is more provocative than the dress," he murmured. "It's different. Addictive."

Sarah found his comment amusing. "Fermented, maybe? My father brought it from the Orient a long time ago. It's called Poppy's Splendor."

He grinned, guided them into a dark corner and slowed almost to a standstill. "I missed you," he said simply. "I thought you'd at least talk to me when Mike called." He would have told her how disappointed he'd been except that something in her eyes stopped him. Gabe hesitated, sensing her mood had changed.

"Don't do this," she begged. "I don't need any more complications in my life. I know you and Sheena went to Kauai together. Mike had me dial. Sheena answered."

He looked puzzled. "We went together, but we didn't *stay* together." The truth was, he'd thought about nothing but Sarah the whole time he'd been gone.

Feeling a need for air, Sarah turned and headed for the open patio. Her head pounded. He wasn't making sense. "I call sharing a hotel room *staying* together."

Gabe trailed her, pausing once to shake hands with someone who greeted him. When Sarah would have stopped on the patio, he placed a hand at the small of her back and kept her moving, past the flickering tiki torches out to the sandy beach. For the life of him, Gabe didn't know what she was talking about. "I thought I'd already explained my relationship to Sheena." It was just old family and business ties. Besides, he didn't want to talk about Sheena.

Sarah wobbled as her three-inch heels sank into the sand.

Gabe propped her up against a nearby palm. His gaze softened. "I know you're angry. But I honestly don't know why. I would rather have been at Mike's game if that's what's eating you. I'm sorry, Sarah."

Sarah turned her head and let a cooling breeze wash over her. "We're the ones who should apologize, Gabe. Mike's timing was bad."

"What do you mean? I told him to call. Granted, I thought he'd call earlier—I didn't know about the pizza party." A smile came and went. "I have to admit—if you two had been much later, I'd have checked with the police. That was me who tripped your answering machine three times." He traced a finger down her cheek. "I'm beginning to understand why you worry. I imagined something terrible had happened to you both."

Sarah braced a hand against the tree trunk. Why was it he could make her believe almost anything? To be fair, she supposed hotel business *could* have kept them together that late. But... Oh, for heaven's sake, why didn't he stand still? Sarah shut her eyes to deal with sudden queasiness and almost missed what he was saying.

"The Grand National Surfing Championship starts next week. I'll be at my beach house off and on until they're over. I mentioned it to you a while ago—wondered if you and Mike might come for the weekend. You said no then, but I thought maybe...maybe you feel differently now."

"No. My answer's still the same."

He frowned. Why was she so upset? Did she think surfing was unsafe? Probably. "I know what you said," he told her, "but Mike won't be surfing. Just watching. Nothing wrong with that, is there?"

Sarah's hands curled into fists at her sides. "I saw all I ever want to see of surfers when I was married. Nothing's changed."

"Really?" He pressed against her, his eyes blazing. "I'd say everything's changed." Burying both hands in her upswept curls, he claimed her lips in a searing kiss. Her perfume filled his nostrils—a heady aphrodisiac invading his senses. Gabe wanted to kiss her until any lingering memories of Farrell Michaels left her for good. He wanted *her.* Lord, how he wanted her! He hadn't realized just how much until now.

Sarah's lips parted involuntarily. Gabe staked his claim with a reckless thrust of his tongue. When her knees trembled and she sagged against him, he gentled his hold on her, and his kiss.

Sarah felt the surf pounding in her ears. Or maybe it was the frenzied beat of her heart or the blood singing through her veins. Reality dimmed. She forgot Farrell, forgot surfing. Her hands brushed the ridges down the front of Gabe's shirt. Two of his onyx studs gave way and her hand recoiled from the heat her fingers encountered. Oblivious to all but a world of textures, Sarah didn't hear a woman's voice in the distance calling Gabe's name.

But Gabe heard and exhaling raggedly, willed his pesky sister-in-law to get lost. But she called again. From the edge of the patio this time.

Gabe leaned his forehead against Sarah's and retreated a space. "What is it, Mariel?" he called. "I'm—" He'd been going to say occupied, or busy, but those terms didn't come close to describing it. "I'm involved," he informed her. Which wasn't the half of it. He didn't remember ever being so affected by any woman.

"I can see that. The whole world can see." The woman on the patio sounded less than amused. She sounded perturbed.

Her tone brought Sarah to her senses. She struggled for release. What were they doing? In a public place, too.

Gabe pressed his lips in a tight line, but he let her go. "Mariel, meet Sarah Michaels. Sarah, my brother's wife." His tone was flat. Clipped.

Sarah focused on a pretty blond woman in a blue dress. An ocean breeze ruffled several layers of chiffon, revealing her to be quite pregnant. That didn't keep the woman from studying Sarah in a haughty manner.

"You've found me, Mariel," Gabe said curtly, buttoning his shirt with steady hands. "Tell me what's so damned important." He reached out and clasped Sarah's wrist to keep her from fleeing. He'd just broken through to what he thought was the real woman, the real Sarah Michaels. Family be damned.

"Layman sent me. Dinner's about to be served. You aren't going to be difficult, are you? Your father will be so annoyed."

Gabe gave a snort. "Tell someone who cares."

"Don't be that way," she begged. "The Maxwells have been planning this night for a long time, and they expect you to be there."

Sarah felt somewhat disconnected. Like an outsider looking in. The woman was wearing sapphires that probably cost as much as Sarah's house. And there was no mistaking her reminder of where Gabe belonged.

"Okay." Gabe shrugged. "Go have someone set a place for Sarah. I want her to meet the rest of the family. This is as good a time as any."

"Gabe!" Mariel sounded shocked. "Really, what are you thinking? *She* can't sit at the head table."

Not only was Sarah's head reeling, but she'd been insulted quite enough. Disengaging her wrist, she lifted her chin and said, "Excuse me, please, I'm going to the ladies' room. You two will have to conduct this family squabble without me." Although it cost much of her flagging energy, she managed to cross the patio with her back straight.

The moment she stepped inside, Sarah encountered a waiter holding a tray of drinks. The bright red of the fruit punch she'd found so refreshing caught her eye. She plucked up a frosted glass and succeeded in cooling her ire with a few swallows before she reached the ladies' lounge.

Gabe watched her disappear, his eyes glacial. "Find her, Mariel. I want you to apologize."

His sister-in-law gasped. "You can't mean that. Where's your brain, Gabe? What if Rainee Talbert of 'The Morning News' witnessed that disgusting display? She wouldn't think twice about linking your name with that nobody."

Gabe had never felt like striking a woman in his life—until now. A muscle jerked in his jaw as he clamped down on his anger. "Sarah Michaels is very much a *somebody*, dearest Mariel. And you had better get used to seeing our names linked. She's the woman I intend to marry." Having made a declaration that surprised even him, Gabe left his sister-in-law gaping. Well, he didn't necessarily mean he was getting married tomorrow. But why was Mariel acting so shocked? The whole family had been hinting lately that it was time for him to settle down. Even his father had brought it up.

Mitzi interrupted Sarah's headlong flight to the ladies' room. She took in her friend's flushed face. "Are you all right?"

"I'm fine. Peachy keen," Sarah said flippantly, looking for a place to deposit the remainder of her punch. "If I thought before I didn't belong here, I know it now."

"Harvey saw you go off with Gabe Parker. He's in a snit." Mitzi grinned. "'Course, I pointed out that what's sauce for the gander is sauce for the goose. And I made it very clear you're dining with us."

Sarah felt her color drain at the thought of food.

"Hey, you look a little peaked. Have you eaten at all today?"

Sarah shook her head, then reached to steady herself on the padded door.

"Hypoglycemia," Mitzi concluded. "Low blood sugar," she clarified when Sarah looked mystified. "Go into the lounge and take a few minutes to relax. I'll snag you a plate."

"Thanks, Mitzi. I won't be long."

"If you aren't out in ten minutes, I'll come looking. Say, you haven't been drinking, have you?" Mitzi's eyes narrowed.

"Only fruit punch," Sarah said. "You know I'm not much of a drinker."

"Yeah, but there's for sure some booze in that stuff. You be careful..." Mitzi's warning was lost in the swish of the door.

Sarah went through a second door and stopped at a porcelain sink. She was splashing cold water on her face when the outer door opened and she heard the unmistakable bell-clear tones of Gabe's sister-in-law. Not wanting to be seen, she plucked up a towel and hurried into the nearest stall.

"Mother Parker," the newcomer complained loudly, "Wade thinks you should try and talk sense into Gabe. Honestly, you should have seen him with that *woman*."

Through the narrow crack in the stall door, Sarah watched the pregnant blonde whisk a compact from her beaded purse and in angry strokes begin to powder her nose. She stifled a sudden urge to laugh. Instead, she climbed up on the seat of the commode to get a look at Gabe's mother. Because it made her dizzy, Sarah slid back down as the older woman spoke.

"Wade should know better than to push Gabe," Mrs. Parker said calmly. "Not even his father, who's the most stubborn man I know, can best him in a test of wills. I learned that when Gabriel was young."

Mariel sniffed. "Wade said this Michaels woman has a child. The boy is one of Gabe's charity cases. Oh, I just know he'll ruin us all if he persists in this nonsense, Mother Parker."

"I rather think the Parkers have withstood worse," Gabe's mother said dryly. "But that may explain Gabe's stubbornness. He loves children. You've seen the way he indulges your two. He really needs one of his own."

"Yes. Wade and I thought when Sheena got back from France..."

Mariel's voice trailed off and Sarah strained to hear.

The older woman's voice was sharp. "Myself, I think Sheena is too... Well, she's so..."

"Spoiled?" Mariel suggested.

"I was going to say immature," Gabe's mother returned. "If you're finished, Mariel, I suggest we go. Tell Wade to relax. I'll speak with Gabe later."

Through a kind of thick fog, Sarah registered their leaving. She let a few minutes pass before she felt steady enough to seek out her friends. She probably did need food. After all, she'd skipped lunch.

Sarah wished she could tell Mrs. Parker what such a talk with Gabe would do to Mike. But a woman of that ilk wouldn't care. In her world, charities came and charities went. Hadn't she known all along this would happen?

Sarah picked her way carefully between the tables. She wouldn't have gone back at all if she'd had any idea how close Mitzi and Sam were to the head table. Blindly Sarah took the chair Mitzi patted.

"Are you better?" Worried eyes scanned her.

"Yes," Sarah lied. But she made the mistake of lifting her lashes as she unfolded her napkin and caught Gabe frowning at her. Sheena sat on his right, Layman to his left. Sarah lowered her gaze too fast and felt the room fade. She didn't know what was wrong, unless it was the heat. Did no one else notice how stifling it was in here?

The elder Maxwell heaved his bulk from his chair, forcing Sarah to look up again. Gabe's gaze bore through her this time. She feigned interest in their host. When Layman gave a sharp rap on his crystal water glass with a knife, Sarah thought the top of her head would fly off.

He hoisted a champagne flute and instantly all talk died. Like magic, similar glasses appeared in front of each guest. A host of waiters moved quickly to fill them.

Sarah couldn't seem to take her eyes from Layman's glass. Light from the chandelier set the pale gold liquid ablaze. A chill pranced up her spine. Why did champagne suddenly seem a bad omen?

"My friends," began Maxwell in a rumbling voice, "it pleases me to see so many celebrating my daughter's coming of age. Actually, our reason for this gathering is twofold. My old friend Dave Parker and I have a very special announcement to make tonight."

Were they announcing an engagement? Sarah didn't think she could bear it. Stricken, her eyes sought Gabe. He was making gestures that she couldn't figure out. Did he want her to meet him in the lobby? Was that it? She smothered a giggle as he made faces, punctuated with wild signals. My, but he was being naughty! No wonder he and Mike got on so well. She snickered again.

Mitzi shot her a dark look.

Sarah covered her mouth and pretended interest in hotels.

"After months of negotiations," Maxwell was saying, "I'm pleased to announce that Dave and I have launched a joint venture. Max-Park. A resort complex on Kauai. There's a mock-up in the lobby. We're aiming for the most luxurious and most profitable resort in the islands. Bigger even than Dave's complex on Maui." Applause drowned his words.

"But that's not all," he continued when the clapping died. "It's no secret how I've envied Dave for having two sons to carry on his business." Layman beamed. "Now that Sheena's quit gallivanting around France, she's agreed to join the firm. What pleases me more—Dave just promised that Gabe will teach her the ropes."

Again the ripple of sound. Layman Maxwell touched his glass to Sheena's, then pulled an astonished Gabe to his feet as he bade everyone drink.

Sarah gripped the table. She missed Gabe's thunderous scowl.

"One other thing before we eat..." Layman waited for silence. "This may be somewhat premature, but if Dave and I have any influence, Gabriel's student may graduate into something permanent—if you get my drift."

From the laughter, it was clear everyone did. Sarah closed her eyes. When she opened them, she discovered that the waiter had placed a large dish of caviar directly in front of her. Abruptly she jumped up and ran from the room. All around her, people were surging to their feet, cheering.

Without knowing how she got there, Sarah found herself in the powder room again running cold water over her wrists. Blessedly the heavy door blocked off the revelry. She felt so terrible she didn't even look up when the door flew open and bounced against the wall.

"Sarah, what in hell is wrong with you?" Gabe grabbed up a towel, wet it and sponged her clammy forehead.

She backed away. "You can't come in here," she stammered. "This is the ladies' room."

"The hell I can't. How long have you been like this? Are you sick?"

It would help if he stood still. She placed a staying hand on his chest. There was something she had to say so he wouldn't mistake her hasty exit. "Truly, truly, I wish you and Sheena a long and happy future." Pleased to have completed that speech, Sarah raised her head high and marched out.

Gabe digested Sarah's words, including the way they ran together. "What have you been drinking?" he asked suspiciously, following her.

"I beg your pardon! Not that it's your business, but I had a very nice fruit punch. Now, why don't you make yourself useful? Call me a cab."

He threw back his head and laughed. "You're a cab." Then taking great care, Gabe guided her through the maze of flowers into the lobby.

"Bad joke." Sarah tripped on the carpet and would have fallen if not for his arm.

"Do you have a wrap?" he asked, pausing near the cloak room. When she indicated the shawl hanging over her arm, he moved them past the curious checker. "Tell me how many *mai tais* you had."

"Not one. I do not imbibe," she said primly, although even to her own ears, her words seemed to miss letters like some of Mike's. Curious.

"Of course you don't." Gabe grinned. "All the same, you won't mind if I run you home?"

Sarah blinked owlishly at him and Gabe realized he'd spoken too fast. He dug in his pocket for keys until he remembered he'd let the valet park his car. Damn, but this woman could addle his brain. Spotting a bellman he knew, he signaled. "Could you have my car brought around?"

"Leaving so soon, sir?" The fellow seemed surprised.

Gabe wrapped his arm more tightly around Sarah's waist. "Yes, Maurice. Mrs. Michaels has had too much, er, punch," he finished lamely.

The bellman's faded blue eyes twinkled. "I imagine that would be planter's punch, sir. I've heard it's deadly. I'll see to your car."

"Not planter's punch," she corrected. She lifted her hand to straighten Gabe's bow tie but, instead, knocked it askew. "Something pretty. Red." Sarah frowned, trying to remember. "Scarlett. Scarlett something."

"Scarlett O'Hara?" Gabe studied her bright nod. "Definitely pretty and red, my innocent," he muttered. "Let's hope you still think that in the morning." Her smile came too easily. Yes, she'd probably regret it tomorrow, but perhaps tonight it wouldn't be so bad for her to unwind just a little. Again Gabe wondered about Sarah's upbringing—and marriage. There seemed so many things she hadn't experienced.

Outside, a young valet held the passenger door open as Gabe helped Sarah into the low-slung automobile. She shut her shawl in the door and found the process of retrieving it hilarious.

Gabe pulled out a money clip and passed a twenty to the valet. He peeled off another and handed it to the hovering bellman. "The lady came with Harvey Denton. Could you ask around and find him? Whatever you do, though, don't mention the fruit punch."

"Roger. Would you like a paper bag, sir?"

Gabe shook his head. "Thanks, but I don't think she's had that many."

Sarah waved a fist full of cassettes under his nose as he slid beneath the wheel. "Classical, Parker? You amaze me. I had you pegged as a rock-and-roll man." That struck her as so funny she couldn't seem to get the cassette she'd selected into the slot.

Gabe drove around the loop and stopped to help her. He winced as the full-blown brass of Dvorak blasted out.

Sarah beamed broadly, lowered the window and sank back, clearly pleased with herself.

Gabe rolled his eyes and discreetly turned the music down. He wondered how on earth he was going to explain Sarah's condition to a sitter. And Mike. What if Mike was still up? That young man missed nothing.

He sighed. But then as Sarah leaned over and pillowed her head on his shoulder all doubt vanished. After all, a man who had just told two of the island's most prominent hoteliers to go take a flying leap should certainly be able to come up with something.

CHAPTER EIGHT

THE MUSIC ESCALATED. Not relishing the thought of being stopped by the police, Gabe turned the volume still lower.

Sarah stirred on his shoulder. Her hair tickled his cheek. He glanced down into her gold-flecked eyes and pictured the two of them riding this way twenty years from now.

She yawned, covered her mouth with one hand and apologized. "I'm sorry. I can't imagine why I'm so sleepy." Her lashes slowly drifted over her eyes again.

Hearing her *s*'s tangle, Gabe smiled. "Sarah, honey, when did you eat last?" he asked gently.

She sat up, eyes clouding. "Dinner, I guess. Yesterday. Why?"

Shaking his head, Gabe stroked his jaw. "No wonder the Scarletts hit you like a ton of bricks."

Sarah leaned forward and popped out the Dvorak tape and switched it for a more mellow piece by Ravel. Her brows knit. "Shouldn't you be off building skyscrapers or something?"

Gabe took a corner too fast. The Porsche swayed.

"Don't," she begged, placing both hands to her temples.

"Don't what?" His mind had already jumped ahead to how he'd handle things once he got her home.

"Don't jerk the car. I don't feel so well."

A wry grin played at the corners of his mouth. "You have my sympathy, sweetheart. I've been bombed a few times myself."

"Bombed?" Her eyelids flickered.

"Tipsy," he said, tugging lightly on an escaped curl. "As in Scarlett O'Haras, love. As in the demon rum. Or in this case, Southern Comfort."

"N...n...no." She shook her head.

"Yep. 'Fraid so." He took a wide swing into her drive, then braked to a stop. "Good news. We're home."

He came around to help her out. But she clung to the seat belt with both hands.

"No. No. My knees won't work."

Patiently he loosened her fingers from the belt. His teeth flashed white in the moonlight. "Are you able to walk, or shall I carry you?"

"Why couldn't I walk?" she demanded as she got out of the car. Even as the words left her lips, she tripped and nearly fell on her face.

Gabe caught her. "Time to get serious, Sarah. Who's your sitter? We need to make up a story. Deal?"

As the cooler night air hit her, Sarah started to laugh.

Gabe steered her toward the front steps, but she released his cummerbund and stole his tie, teasing all the while. "Too stuffy," she scolded, wagging an unsteady finger under his nose. "Harvey's stuffy. Not Gabriel." She leaned into his chest, looked into his face and grinned seductively. He was having trouble being serious himself. Maybe because he liked the way she said his name. And the way her eyes sparkled in the moonlight.

She popped the top two studs on his shirt and kicked out of her strappy shoes. Dangling them on one finger, she tickled him with his tie.

Gabe had never seen her in such a playful mood, and he had little resistance. Catching her around the waist, he kissed her soundly on the lips, and then it was his turn to chuckle as she looked astounded.

But his victory was short-lived. She tossed everything she held over her shoulder and threaded her fingers through his hair. "Dance with me," she insisted.

As she hummed off-key, he waltzed her a few steps across the soft grass. Her rich laughter triggered a sudden tightness in his stomach. All Gabe knew was that he wanted to hear her laugh like this more often. Pulling her close, he vowed she would. His lips sought hers, no longer teasing.

The front door opened, spilling light across the lawn. A hesitant voice called into the darkness, "Who's there? Mrs. Michaels? Is that you?" The porch light flared.

Sarah jerked away at the sound. "Jenny Sue?" Light struck her in the eyes. She buried her head in Gabe's shoulder.

Executing a fancy dip, he snatched up the items Sarah had dropped. The cummerbund and tie he stuffed into a jacket pocket. He handed her the shoes.

"Mrs. Michaels isn't feeling well. Flu, maybe. I'm Gabe Parker... a friend. I drove her home."

"Oh, hey," the girl said, opening the door wider. "I feel like I know you, Mr. Parker. Mike talked about nothing else." She frowned. "You know, he wasn't himself this evening. Complained about his stomach. He even went to bed early. I guess he has the flu, too."

Gabe chewed at the inside of his mouth and thought about that for a moment. Humming again, Sarah hadn't heard. Now she nipped playfully at Gabe's ear, then skipped nimbly out of his reach. Flinging her arms wide, she pretended to swoop and soar like a bird.

As she circled behind him, Gabe grabbed for her. "What in blue blazes are you doing?" he hissed. "I told that girl you're sick."

"I'm a bird. I'm a plane. I'm Wonder Woman," Sarah chortled, tweaking his shirt collar, enjoying his obvious distress.

"Have a heart, Sarah," he breathed. "Come on. Make like you're Wonder Woman with the flu."

"Is she all right?" Jenny Sue called.

"What happened to sleepy?" he murmured near Sarah's ear. More loudly, he answered the sitter, "Do you think maybe you could turn back her bed?"

"Sure," Jenny Sue agreed, quickly withdrawing.

Gabe reeled Sarah in slowly, unsure what she'd do next. He noticed then that she looked pale. He suggested she lean on him, and they made it into the house as the baby-sitter reappeared.

Gabe whisked Sarah down the hall past Jenny Sue. He all but shoved her into her bedroom and said in an undertone, "Stay put. Please!"

"Should I call my mom?" the teenager asked uncertainly.

"She'll be fine." Gabe pulled out his wallet. "How much does she owe you? I'll take care of it and see you home. I'll square with her later." Just now, he couldn't get Sarah's sitter out of there soon enough.

"It's not much." The girl began to gather her school books. "I know she planned to be later. I'm sorry her evening was ruined." She shrugged. "Mrs. Michaels doesn't go out often, and I've never seen her look so great."

The bills Gabe had dug out quivered as he held them. "Yes," he agreed, remembering. "She looked very beautiful." Better, though, was hearing her laugh, he realized as he handed over the money.

"This is too much," Jenny Sue protested. "It's just past midnight."

"If I know that scamp Mike, you earned it. Come on. I'll see you home."

"You don't need to. I only live two doors down."

"All the same, it's dark. I'd want someone to see you inside if you were my daughter." Something else had just hit Gabe—he'd always thought someday he'd have a houseful of boys. Now his subconscious added a girl, a miniature version of Sarah. He shook his head, but the idea remained.

The sitter grinned and headed for the door Gabe had left standing ajar. "Parents," she said. "You're all alike. Overprotective."

"Interesting observation, but I'm not a parent—yet." It occurred to him that he didn't know if Sarah even wanted more children. Quietly he closed the door. Much less sure of the rosy future he'd always taken for granted, he followed the girl.

There was a lot he didn't know about Sarah, but twice as much she didn't know about him. Tomorrow they'd start swapping life stories—and other things, like a few more of those steamy kisses.

"This is it." Jenny Sue pointed out a neat white single-story structure, with a porch light shining. "You don't have to come to the door. My mom'll be up." She pulled a wry face. "She always is."

"Would you rather have parents who didn't care?" Gabe's father, gone on business so much, loomed in his mind. His mother, more like Sarah, ran a tight ship. Grandpa Parker had been his real anchor.

"You're just as nice as Mike said," Jenny Sue blurted. "Say, are you sure Mrs. Michaels will be okay there by herself?"

"I plan on sticking around for a bit." Gabe hesitated. "So you squelch neighborhood rumors if my car is there into the wee hours, okay?"

"My mom will. She hates gossip," Jenny Sue said. "'Bye." Waving, she disappeared inside.

What a nice child, Gabe thought, jogging back to Sarah's. He'd make it a point to meet her parents sometime and tell them. Lately he'd come to see that being a parent wasn't always as straightforward as it might seem. Being a single parent was downright difficult. Sarah was doing a better job than she gave herself credit for.

Inside Sarah's home again, Gabe stripped off his jacket and rolled up his sleeves. Tomorrow maybe he'd take Sarah and Mike to meet his mother. He doubted if they'd find his dad at home. Just now he needed to get some food into her. However, first he'd better let her know he was back.

He tapped on the bedroom door. "Sarah," he called softly. Nothing. Not so much as a murmur. Waiting briefly, Gabe pushed the door open a crack. She lay curled on the bed, sound asleep, her head pillowed in the crook of one arm. Jade satin shimmered around her beneath the bright overhead light. Tender feelings welled up and tripped over themselves on the way to Gabe's heart. Dropping down beside her, he put a hand on her arm. "Sarah," he said, quietly, "you need to get up and out of that dress."

Her eyes flickered briefly, then closed as if weighted.

Gabe rubbed the back of his neck. "Now what?" he muttered, half under his breath. Restless, he got up and opened her closet. Right off, he spied the robe she had on the other night. He laid it carefully beside her and pulled out dresser drawers until he found her nightclothes. He'd kind of figured her for the cotton-gown, little-pastel-flower type. A much washed, stretched out, oversize nightshirt showed Gabe how unpredictable she was. And it was inscribed with a most unlikely slogan. My Life is Filled with Romance, Lust, Danger and Dust Balls the Size of Tumbleweeds. He chuckled to himself, placed it with the robe and left to make coffee.

He carried her cup into the bedroom to find that she hadn't moved a muscle. Nor did efforts to interest her in coffee succeed. All she did was mumble and roll over.

At last Gabe gave up, drew the covers over her and drank the coffee himself. According to Sarah's bedside clock, it was closing fast on one. Should he go or stay? He couldn't decide.

He yawned and went back for another cup of the Kona blend that was his favorite. Returning to the living room, he sat in the recliner and picked up a book with dog-eared pages. *How to Win at Parenting.* Funny, he'd always assumed parents won by default. He read the first few chapters, paying close attention to the notes Sarah had penciled in the margins. They said things like "good idea, can't afford." That was beside a paragraph about getting your child a puppy. He smiled. Meticulous as she was, he couldn't picture her with a dog.

Gabe was engrossed in the chapter on single parenting when he heard Mike cry out for Sarah. Doubting that Sarah would hear, he hurried down the hall to the boy's room. Light spilling from a Ninja Turtle night-light bathed the room in an eerie green glow. Mike was all but hidden beneath stuffed animals.

Not wanting to frighten him, Gabe spoke softly from the doorway. "Mike, it's Gabe. I gave your mom a lift home from the party, kicker. Do you need her, or can I help?"

He heard restless thrashing, more sobbing and an almost garbled plea for Sarah. Gabe realized then the child was talking in his sleep. He stepped into the room and walked to the bed, hoping to wake him from the throes of a nightmare.

At first, Gabe thought Mike was feverish. Sweat dampened his fine blond hair. A hand to the brow revealed that his skin was cold. Clammy. Now Gabe could see that he was curled into a tight fetal ball, both hands pressed to his stomach. Even in the muted light, he saw where recent tears had streaked colorless cheeks. Gabe flipped on the bedside lamp and lost no time shaking the child awake.

"Mike, Mike. Talk to me, kicker. Are you in pain? Show me where you hurt."

"G-Gabe?" Mike blinked in the brightness, but the eyes he turned on the man were dark. Unfocused. "Wh-where's Mommy?"

The plea tore through Gabe's heart. In the weeks since they'd met he'd never known Mike to be less than tough. Grown-up. He didn't say "Mommy."

"Mike, listen to me. Your mom is sleeping. How long have you been like this? Do any of your friends at school have the flu?"

Mike scrubbed his eyes with one hand. "I felt okay this afternoon. Don't know if anybody else is sick. Gabe...it hurts bad."

Gabe chewed at the inside of his mouth. He thought of one other thing. "Did you and your sitter eat a lot of junk food tonight? I know my brother and I used to pig out whenever the folks went out for the evening."

Mike shook his head. "Mom left money for pizza. Jenny Sue ate it. I didn't want any." A big tear found its way between his freckles.

No pizza? This was more serious than Gabe had thought. Maybe appendix. Lord, he hoped not. "Show me exactly where you hurt. Can you do that?"

The boy attempted to straighten his legs, but cried out and grabbed his stomach high on the left side. Soundless tears rolled down his cheeks.

Gabe swore under his breath and cast a glance toward Sarah's room. He could drive Mike to emergency, but by whose authority? Because they weren't related, he doubted anyone would accept his permission to treat the child. Then Mike whimpered again. "Don't try moving, Mike. Let me get your mother. It'll be all right. I promise." Yet as he made his way next door, Gabe wasn't nearly so confident. He'd read somewhere that pain from appendicitis occasionally radiated to the left side, but he thought it stayed low in the abdomen. Mike seemed fairly consistent in holding his hands high, just under his rib cage.

He threw open her door and switched on the bedside lamp. Sarah was beginning to stir. "Mike?" she said, squinting, "is that you?"

"It's Gabe. I need you, Sarah." His voice was raw, urgent.

Sarah sat up fast and clutched the covers beneath her chin. "What are you doing in my bedroom?" she hissed, putting a hand to her reeling head.

About that time Mike cried out for her again. She threw the covers aside and got her feet tangled in the sheets. She almost fell, but Gabe caught her. "Let go," she said, struggling. "What's wrong? I've never heard him cry like that!"

Gabe supported her with a firm hand around her waist. "I've been trying to tell you, Sarah. He's sick. He's crying with stomach pains."

She jerked from his hold and discovered she was still wearing her gown. Her eyes clouded in memory. She said, "Maybe he has the flu."

"I don't think so, Sarah. But he needs a doctor. I'll go sit with him while you get dressed and call your doctor. Tell him to meet us at the hospital. Then I'll drive you there."

"I want to see him myself." She straightened her dress and started for the door.

"Let me get him. You're shaking and you look like a ghost. That won't help him. Trust me, Sarah."

"All right." Her voice was steady, but just barely. "Give me five minutes."

"It'll be all right, Sarah. If it's his appendix, they'll take it out. If it's something else, they'll find out what."

"Wh-what time is it?" she asked.

"Almost one-thirty," he said, checking his watch.

"Why are you still here? Where's Jenny Sue?"

"Later, Sarah. Go. Dress."

As she went, Gabe realized what a tight rein he had on his emotions. He wanted to drive away the anxiety he'd seen lurking deep in her eyes. He wanted her to trust him, dammit! Mike cried out again, forcing him to put those particular feelings on a back burner. There was no doubt that his heart was involved here. He could wait to find out about hers.

True to her word, Sarah popped into Mike's bedroom door in five minutes. Pale, but efficient, she pressed a kiss to his cheek and slid a thermometer under his arm. "It's below normal," she announced a minute later.

"What'd the doctor say?" Gabe asked.

"They're paging him. His answering service wanted me to call back with the temperature reading."

She left to do that while Gabe dug out Mike's Batman slippers. The boy said he didn't have a robe, so Gabe helped him into his jacket. They were going to the hospital. Gabe didn't care what the answering service said.

Sarah came back. "Dr. Manolo will meet us at St. Jude's. But you don't have to go," she told Gabe coolly. "I can manage."

Gabe's answer was to gather the boy carefully up in his arms and strike out for his car. "You hold him," he said when Sarah followed. "I'll drive."

Gabe backed out and headed toward Pearl Harbor. Concentrating on his driving, he only half heard Mike's constant jabbering.

"Me and the guys played soccer out in the backyard today, Gabe, but I didn't do so good. I let Jim Cline get three goals. Once him and me crashed together hard. After that, he just runned faster than me."

"Ran," Sarah corrected automatically, smoothing a lock of hair out of his eyes. "Why don't you hush?" she said softly, placing a kiss on his forehead. "Puts you in a sweat thinking about soccer."

"Wait." Gabe frowned. "Tell us about that accident with Jim. Did you fall? Did he land on top of you?" He turned to Sarah. "Jim outweighs him by a good twenty pounds."

Mike caught his breath in pain. "Jim was goin' fast. He plowed into me with his head. I didn't fall, 'cause I whammed into Cubby Burke."

Sarah turned her head and looked at Gabe. Quick moves still made her woozy. "What is it?" she asked. "You think he might have internal injuries? Oh, my Lord." She cradled her son tenderly. "I knew I shouldn't have gone to that party."

"I didn't say that, Sarah," Gabe cautioned. "We need all the facts. I think it's important to tell the doctor what happened with the boys."

Mike moaned and burrowed deeper into his mother's arms.

"Can't you hurry?" she begged, her face ashen, her eyes teary.

"We're almost there," he said, sounding calmer than his rapid pulse suggested. "Getting stopped for speeding wouldn't be in our best interests."

"No," Sarah agreed meekly. "What kind of injury would cause these symptoms, do you think?"

He remembered a football player he knew in college who had taken a hit in the lower back. "I'm not a doctor," he muttered, but Gabe recalled they'd had to surgically remove his friend's spleen.

"You brought it up," Sarah said, sounding perplexed.

"How old were you when you lost your mother?" he asked to change the subject. Not a good choice, he immediately realized.

"Fifteen," she said woodenly.

Gabe winced. "Rough. But you still had your father, right?"

Her words came as if from a distance. "Dad had just accepted a two-year tour of duty overseas. He thought I'd be better off staying here. He hired an ex-army nurse to help. She was strict and she didn't much like kids. By the time his tour was over we'd both changed. I was no longer a grief-stricken needy adolescent, and he'd been without family for too long."

Gabe's heart squeezed. "Look," he said, "here's the hospital." They found the emergency entrance and he pulled into the adjacent parking lot for hospital personnel only. "I'll carry him, then move the car."

"Don't want no doctor," Mike whimpered. "Gabe, stay. I'm scared."

Gabe made the transfer from Sarah's arms to his as smoothly as possible, but Mike still cried out.

Sarah wasn't moving very fast herself. She pressed her lips tight and walked with purpose. Already, her head was beginning to pound. And she must look a mess, she thought.

A fact confirmed by the expression on the face of the nurse at the desk. Sarah steadied herself on the counter, saying in a not-so-steady voice, "We have Farrell Michaels to see Dr. Manolo. Is he here yet?"

"Not yet," the hard-eyed nurse replied. She shoved a clipboard and some forms at Sarah. "If you'd like to fill these out, Mrs. Michaels, I can take your husband and son back into a room."

Sarah put a hand to her head and gazed helplessly at Gabe. "I, ah, that is..." She blushed. "We're not married."

The nurse, a matronly woman, lifted a brow. "Oh. I see," she said.

"No," Gabe broke in, taking command. "I don't think you do. I suggest you take all three of us to the room, then she'll fill out your papers." Let them tow the damned car. He didn't care.

Sarah flashed him a grateful smile. So this was the Gabe his mother had said couldn't be bested in a test of wills. She closed her eyes and took a deep breath, glad he was on her side. On Mike's side, she corrected.

Gabe knew what this whole effort must be costing her. She had spunk, but he'd bet anything her head was churning like a cement mixer. He'd seen people run on adrenaline before. When they ran out, they crashed. He hoped the doctor came before that happened.

The nurse led them to a spotless room and stiffly told Sarah to remove Mike's outer clothing. "I'll be back for the forms and to take his temperature." It was the last they saw of her. Shortly thereafter, Dr. Manolo arrived. Gabe had just watched Sarah shakily sign the final release.

Like Gabe, Mike's doctor was dressed in formal wear. Except that his was immaculate, where Gabe's was now hopelessly rumpled.

"Well, Sarah," the physician said briskly, "let's have a look at this young man."

"Sorry to disturb your evening, Doctor." Sarah moved to the opposite side of the examining table as she spoke. "It looks as if we took you away from something important."

"I'd only just arrived home from the party I believe you left earlier. The Maxwell gathering." The two men shook hands and exchanged names. Dr. Manolo immediately shucked his jacket, rolled up his sleeves and scrubbed with liquid soap. All the while, he joked quietly with Mike. Without asking direct questions, he managed to get the facts about the soccer accident, as well as Mike's symptoms.

The doctor wasn't far into the physical examination when he ran a hand over Mike's left side, and the child let out a sharp cry. Dr. Manolo straightened. "I'll need to get X rays and have some blood drawn," he said. "I suspect the collision he had may have injured his spleen."

Gabe passed a hand over his stubbled jaw. It was what he'd feared.

Sarah blanched, clasped her hands and put them to her lips. "Spleen?" Her voice shook. She didn't object when Gabe stepped around the table and placed a warm hand on her neck. "That sounds serious," she murmured.

"Now, now," the doctor cautioned, "let's see the extent of the damage before you go falling apart. Mr. Parker, could you go to the X-ray department with the boy? I'd like a word with Sarah." Opening the door, he called for a nurse.

Gabe looked to Sarah for approval. She barely had time to nod before a woman in white breezed in and whisked Mike's gurney away. Gabe had to jog to keep up.

It seemed to Sarah that she'd no more than finished giving Dr. Manolo background information when the two returned.

"You'd have been proud of him, Sarah," Gabe said. Turning to Mike, he prompted, "Show your mother the badge they gave you for courage."

"I hurt," the little boy sniffled. "I don't wanna be brave. I wanna go home. Gabe—take me home."

"You be brave a little longer," Dr. Manolo advised, patting him on the hand. "I'll go take a peek at those films and be back in a jiffy."

When he left, Gabe joined Sarah. "You okay?" he asked.

"I can't think. My mouth feels dry as sand and my mind won't work. Whatever must Dr. Manolo think of me? I couldn't answer half the things he asked about my family history. I know next to nothing about Farrell's."

Gabe pulled her close and rubbed his chin over her hair. "Don't sweat it. He expects you to be nervous."

"I am, Gabe. What will they do?" she whispered. "Not surgery?"

He straightened. "Did the doctor say that?"

"Only in passing," she mumbled, smiling at Mike as she left Gabe's arms and stroked her son's hair.

The doctor returned. Sarah reached for Gabe's hand without thinking.

"Well," Dr. Manolo said, ignoring her alarm, "it's the spleen, all right. Enlarged." He held a gray film up to the light. "Probably bruised."

Sarah turned to look, and she shrank from the bright light.

"White blood count doesn't suggest there's any bleeding into the abdominal cavity. That's good. Excellent, in fact," the doctor went on. "We don't like taking the spleen out of children. We're beginning to think it's a defense mechanism against infection, even though it's not essential to life. I'm ordering a shot. Anti-inflammatory. If that doesn't do the trick, I'll consider placing him on a low dose of steroids."

"So he can go home?" Sarah questioned, slipping a reassuring arm around the child's thin shoulders.

The doctor tapped a pen on the table. "Can you keep him quiet? No activity other than trips to the bathroom for a week. No soccer for the rest of the school year. If he takes it up again, you'd better see he gets some protective shields to wear. Next time, he might not be this lucky."

Mike started to cry and Sarah tried soothing him.

"Hey, kicker," Gabe said, bending over him, "part of a year isn't so bad. They bench the pros longer than that sometimes." Lacing his fingers with Sarah's, he continued, "I've got a great idea. Quit fussing and maybe your mom will let you come stay at my beach house next week. I'll put a lounger on the patio. You can be lazy all day and watch the surfers qualify for the Grand Nationals. How does that sound?"

Sarah sputtered as Mike scrubbed at his eyes, and tried to smile. "All right!"

Dr. Manolo grinned. "Sounds like a good deal to me. Mind if I make a house call? I haven't seen the big competition in years. Got a few medals myself before med school." He looked sheepish then and shrugged.

"You're welcome, of course," Gabe offered. "Maybe if you tell his mother surfing's respectable, she'll come Friday and spend the weekend with him herself."

Sarah didn't reply. Not to the doctor's comments, or to Gabe's. She gave the doctor a cool thanks and asked which hip he needed for Mike's shot.

"Left," he said. "I'll give it myself. Why don't you let Mr. Parker steady Mike's hands? I don't want him wiggling."

"I've managed for eight years without Mr. Parker, Doctor. Mike won't wiggle."

Gabe noticed the measurable drop in room temperature. He knew the way Sarah felt about surfing had to do with her ex. Precisely what, he wasn't sure. Her dislike of surfers must run deeper than he'd thought. It definitely didn't help his case when Mike begged to sit on his lap during the shot. By the time they left the emergency room, Sarah's short terse responses dripped icicles.

They were back at Sarah's home and had Mike tucked into bed—with a promise from Gabe that he'd definitely be back for him the next day—before Sarah asked to speak to him.

Gabe didn't like her tone.

"Mike will not be going to your beach house," she said coldly. "Not tomorrow. Not ever. I appreciate all you've done tonight, but I suggest you call him tomorrow with a plausible reason for changing your mind."

"Why, Sarah? I'd never let anything happen to him. I heard the doctor's orders. You said yourself Mike minds me better than he does you."

"That's another thing," she said. "With soccer out, you can taper off your visits. It'll give you more time to teach Sheena."

Gabe's eyes blazed. "Just like that?" He snapped his fingers. "You expect me to fade out of Mike's life? And yours? Somehow, you know Sheena's not the issue here. Tell me what's really bugging you."

"I don't like surfing, or surfers. If that's not clear enough, hear this—I don't like being manipulated. How dare you invite my son to your beach house when I'd already said no?"

"Tell me why he can't come. Am I being blamed for another man's sins, Sarah? I'm *not* Farrell. I understand he did a real number on you and Mike, and I understand how you feel about him. Why did you marry the guy if he was such a bastard?"

Her hands balled into fists at her sides. "I wasn't as smart then as I am now."

"Marriage doesn't just happen, Sarah. It takes two. There must have been *something* positive that came from it?"

"My son!" she shouted. "Now, go. Please. I have a raging headache."

"I'm sure you do." He yanked her up against his chest. His eyes gleamed in the subdued lamplight. "Did you drink too many pretty red drinks at some other party and wake up married? Is that it?"

"Certainly not. Get your hands off me. I don't like you touching me."

"Ah, at last the truth. You married for sex, but it was lousy, huh? Well, you've compared me to your ex in every other way. Maybe you'd like to see how I stack up in that department before you compare scores."

The kiss, born of his anger, changed to desire before Gabe's lips even touched hers. By the time his hands slid around her slender rib cage and up her rigid backbone, he didn't want to fight anymore. He never had. Yet he needed some indication of Sarah's feelings for him, so he poured everything into the kiss, begging her for a response.

She gave none.

Backed against a door where they'd ended, he released her instantly. Her utter passivity forced him to do that. Considering what she'd been through, he felt like a first-class heel.

Her eyes were haunted and dark. An apology that erupted from his heart lodged in Gabe's lungs. His throat worked and his fingers curled into his sides. "Sarah—" He got no further.

Sarah rubbed her arms where his fingers had left warm imprints on her icy skin. "Oh, you compare all right, Gabriel Parker," she informed him. "Nothing mattered to Farrell, either, except what *he* wanted. Please, just leave. Leave me and my son alone. Get yourself a new community project."

"Sarah, it's not like that." He spread his palms. "Listen, I beg you!"

She stood, unmoving and unmoved.

Gabe turned away. She looked as if her nerves were stretched so tight she'd break at the slightest provocation rather than bend. Lord, how he cared about her and Mike! But if she didn't know by now that he wasn't like her ex-husband, there was nothing left for him to do but retreat. "Go to bed," he said gently, turning back to cup her cheek with a hand that wasn't quite steady. "I'll let myself out."

"You do that," she said, avoiding his touch. "I meant what I said. Don't come back—or it'll be Mike who's hurt in the end."

Gabe closed his eyes and rubbed a thumb across his tired brow. They were both drained, and things always looked better in daylight. "This isn't over, Sarah. I was trying to help. You saw how upset Mike was about giving up soccer. Please reconsider before you set up a no-win situation." He picked up the book on parenting that had fallen open on the floor when Mike had cried out and shoved it into her hands. "Here. You underlined the answer." Without a backward glance, he grabbed his wrinkled tuxedo jacket and left.

Sarah glanced at the passage. "Children thrive best in an atmosphere of love and trust." She threw the book down and went to check on Mike.

THE SUN WAS already high in the sky the next morning when Gabe realized he'd been watching twenty-foot waves pound the shore at Waimea Bay for almost two hours. In all that time he'd come to only one clear conclusion— Sarah wasn't likely to change her mind about surfing. He wouldn't press her further to take Mike to Sunset Beach.

That would give her a week to think things through. The big problem was figuring how to let Mike down easy. Gabe wasn't sure he had the finesse. But Sarah was right, it wasn't his place to have made the suggestion again without first asking her. At least not yet. Come next Sunday, though, when the Grand Nationals ended, one way or another they'd settle what was between them. And he'd be damned if he'd leave her alone until they did.

CHAPTER NINE

THE TELEPHONE SHRILLED. Sarah pulled the covers over her head to block the sound. Slowly she opened one eye, groped about for the phone and knocked it onto the floor. The noise ripped through her head.

"H-hello," she stammered, at last getting it to her ear.

"Sarah?" Mitzi sounded hesitant. "I didn't wake you, did I?"

"Isn't it Sunday? Why are you calling so early?" she croaked.

"Early? Sarah, it's eleven o'clock."

Sarah wet her parched lips. "Eleven," she repeated tonelessly. "And Mike isn't up? Oh, no." Panic seized her. "Hold on. Or shall I call back?"

"I'll hold."

Sarah stood with some effort. On legs wobbly as a toddler's, she made her way next door. She was delighted to see Mike sitting up in bed, TV blaring.

He saw her and waved.

Then Sarah noticed that his coverlet was a jumble of small stacks of clean clothing. "What's with all the laundry, mister?"

"Not laundry, Mom. I'm gettin' stuff ready for when Gabe comes."

Sarah put a hand to her head. She brushed a pile aside and sat heavily on the end of his bed and tried for a reasonable tone. "Dr. Manolo said you needed rest."

Mike's lips pressed in a stubborn line. "He said I could go with Gabe."

Sarah's latest argument with Gabe ricocheted around inside her head. How could she explain to an eight-year-old that the man he idolized shared too many undesirable traits with his footloose father?

She couldn't. Not yet. Not until her head stopped whirling like a windmill. "I, uh . . . I left your aunt Mitzi waiting on the phone, Mike. I wanted to see how you were feeling."

"Better." He rubbed a hand over his ribs. "Don't got no pain today, not 'less I move quick."

"Any. You don't have *any* pain. 'Don't got no' is a double negative."

He tilted his head, gave her a squinty look and promptly changed the subject. "I'm hungry. When's breakfast?"

"Breakfast?" The thought made her stomach churn. "What would you like?" she asked.

"Chocolate chip pancakes," he said without hesitation.

"Ugh." She couldn't prevent her involuntary shudder.

"They're good." Suddenly he looked contrite. "Now I 'member—last night Gabe said you didn't feel good. Are you still sick, Mom?"

Sarah recalled just enough to make her uncomfortable with his question. "Better," she assured him. "Hey, if I don't go back and talk with Mitzi, she'll think we both died."

"Okay. Holler when it's breakfast."

"I'll bring yours," she promised, making good her escape.

Back in her room, Sarah snatched up the phone. "Mitzi?"

"I was about to send out the National Guard. Is everything all right? Sarah, are you hung over?" When there was a lengthy pause on Sarah's end, Mitzi chuckled. "Well, I did urge you to hang loose, didn't I? So, tell me—did Gabe spend the night? You'll have to hurry, though. I told Osamu I was calling to remind you about my trip to Mother's family reunion. I couldn't wait a whole week to find out if you . . . well, you know . . ."

Scenes from last night's party, and after, flashed through Sarah's mind in splashes of brilliant technicolor.

"Well?" Mitzi said impatiently. "Does the pregnant pause mean he's there? That you did?"

"It does not," Sarah said when she found her voice. "It means I forgot you were going to San Francisco. I intended to ask your mom to baby-sit Mike next week. He got hurt playing soccer yesterday. What Gabe and I did was spend half the night in the emergency room." She paused, then said wryly, "But I'm afraid you're right about my condition, Mitzi. I can't even think straight."

"Back up," Mitzi said. "How badly is Mike hurt?"

"He collided with another boy and bruised his spleen. Spleenalomegaly, Dr. Manolo called it. It could have been worse—if it had ruptured."

"That happened to one of Osamu's wrestlers last year. Wow! It can't have been a fun evening. I was worried because Harvey said you'd been treating Scarlett O'Haras like fruit punch."

Sarah muttered, "I thought they *were* fruit punch."

"Only you, Sarah. Only you. Must have been rough doing the hospital run after that."

"Gabe helped." She stopped, realizing that was an understatement.

"Aren't you lucky it was Gabe who took you home and not Harvey?"

Sarah frowned. Lucky for *Mike*. Viewed from that perspective, she'd probably been too hard on Gabe. After all, what would she have done without him?

"Yo, Sarah? You still there?" Mitzi raised her voice. "Hey, have you thought of asking Gabe to keep Mike next week? He's his own boss."

"He offered," Sarah said lightly. "Of course I didn't accept."

"Why not? Are you nuts? Mike would love it."

Sarah winced. "Must you shout?"

"Sorry. If you refused, I guess you have a good reason."

"Yes. He's a judge in some surfing contest and he'd expected to keep Mike at his beach house all week. Can't you just imagine the kind of supervision any child, let alone a sick one, would get in that atmosphere?"

"Sarah, I swear. How long are you going to flog a dead horse? You just admitted Gabe stuck with you last night. Would Farrell have done as much?"

"No." Sarah had no illusions about her ex-husband. "If it was anything but surfing, Mitzi..." Old memories swam through Sarah's head.

"Darn, Sam's calling me. We have to go pick up Mother and get to the airport." Mitzi sounded unhappy. "Sarah, I love you dearly, but you have to wake up and smell the flowers. I saw the way Gabe Parker looked at you last night. I also heard him tell off his dad, Layman, *and* dear Sheena. Before you throw away something good, you'd better think long and hard. That's positively all I'm going to say, though."

Sarah bit her lip, recalling suddenly how much she'd missed Gabe the night Mike's team had won and they'd gone for pizza. Recalling how much she like his touch, his kisses. Liked them too much. And when that nurse mistook them for husband and wife—well, she'd wished it was true.

"You may be right, Mitzi. I promise to think about it while you're gone. You have a good time on your trip. Send Mike a postcard from Fisherman's Wharf, would you?"

When Mitzi had hung up, Sarah clutched the receiver for several moments, deep in thought. Sometime when she hadn't been looking, her once-dormant passion had been stirred by Gabe Parker. Feelings of respect, of affection, of...something more, had sneaked in and nested in her heart. It wasn't for Mike's sake that she'd become so critical of Gabe, comparing him to Farrell. It was for hers. She knew that it was cowardly. But what if she gave her heart again and the same thing happened? No one, not Mitzi or Lou, *no one* knew how Farrell had destroyed her self-esteem. Little by little she had won it back. And yes, she was treading carefully this time.

Mulling over all that had happened since the arrival of Gabe Parker in their lives, she wandered out to the kitchen. Mitzi had a valid point. It was wrong to lash out at Gabe because her old reactions to Farrell were kicking in. By the time her coffee perked, Sarah had a loose apology formulated. She fine-tuned it as she fixed Mike's chocolate-chip pancakes.

Gabe's offer to keep Mike was, no doubt, genuine. Yet the fact remained that she wasn't comfortable with his plan. The book Gabe had handed her was big on compromise, as well as on love and trust. So, what if she overrode her discomfort and took Mike to Sunset just for the weekend? It was a start.

Pleased with her decision, Sarah smiled. Anytime now, Gabe would call and she would tell him. Whistling softly, she carried a tray to Mike. The stacks of things on his bed were a sobering reminder that she had yet to deal with his disappointment.

"Guess what I just saw on TV, Mom?"

Sarah's breath caught as he turned bright blue eyes, so like Gabe's, eagerly her way. "What did you see?" she teased, scooting one of the piles of shorts aside. "A funny cartoon?"

"Sunset Beach," he announced, accepting the tray and promptly digging into a gooey chip-laden pancake. "I yelled for you," he mumbled with his mouth full. "Guess you didn't hear. They showed Gabe's house. I got to see the patio where I'll be. Golly, Mom, it's right on the ocean. And you know what?" he rushed on, ignoring her meager protest. "They showed him doin' all this neat stuff. Did you know he tests the sea for org'nisms? Bad org'nisms that spill outa ships and stuff. The man 'splained how surfers all over are doin' this for the 'virement. What's 'virement, Mom?"

"I think he meant environment, Mike. Our natural resources—land, water, air. You know how I told you plastics and pollutants are ruining our water and our air? And how, because we live on an island, we have to be especially careful?''

Sarah was actually shocked to hear Gabe and other surfers cared about the environment. It certainly wasn't anything that ever entered Farrell's mind. "Don't talk with your mouth full," she told Mike as he began to speak.

"Sorry." Mike chewed fast and swallowed. "Gabe must be pretty 'portant to be on TV, don'cha think?"

"Important, Mike." Sarah frowned. "Yes," she said slowly, digesting that bit of truth. "Gabe comes from a successful and important family."

Sarah remembered then how his sister-in-law had called her a nobody. Had she really been so foolish as to entertain exploring a relationship with him? There were other issues between them besides her dislike of surfing. More important ones. Kisses, feelings, meant nothing compared to social standing. More than once Gabe had made remarks that inadvertentlly pointed out their differences. Goodness, he owned yachts, and she didn't know from one year to the next if she could pay her property taxes!

"Mike, I need to wash my hair. Will you be okay?" Sarah was too shaken by the discovery to listen to any more hero worship. "Leave the tray on your nightstand when you finish. I'll pick it up later."

"But you never said when Gabe's gonna be here," Mike protested.

"I don't know." Her tone was sharp. "Being on TV and all, he may forget." It would be infinitely easier all around if Gabe ended his volunteer work now. Doing it later would be much harder on Mike. On *her.* So here they were, back at square one.

Mike stubbornly held faith. "He won't forget, Mom. Gabe always does what he says."

Bully for Gabe. Sarah stalked down the hall and into the bathroom. Feelings for Gabriel Parker that had soared briefly were suddenly jerked up short again. Nothing had changed. What she couldn't allow was for Mike to be left dangling in the middle. Somehow, she had to find the backbone to end this once and for all.

She closed her eyes and stepped into the shower. If only it wasn't so difficult. She hadn't thought Mike would miss Farrell, whom he'd hardly known, but the questions had started when he went to school and discovered most of his classmates had *two* parents. There was no doubt in her mind that Gabe filled a gaping void in her son's life.

Clean hair made Sarah feel almost human again. However, no great revelation had come to her in the pulsing massage of the spray. It fact, it was downright frustrating that every thought doubled back to Gabriel Parker.

The doorbell chimed. Sarah's heart raced. They rarely had visitors on Sunday. Unless Gabe had decided to drop by, instead of calling. The possibility slowed her steps. She wasn't ready to see him yet.

Mike's door flew open. "Bet that's Gabe." His voice rose excitedly.

"You get back into bed. I'll check." Sarah crossed to look through the peephole. "It's Harvey," she told Mike, reaching for the doorknob, surprised herself.

Harvey slicked one hand through his hair, then stepped inside. "I hope I'm not disturbing you, Sarah."

She didn't respond, only gathered her bathrobe close and retied the belt.

"I was on my way to Sunday brunch and decided to stop by and see how you are." He angled his chin and tugged at the knot of his paisley tie.

"I'm fine, Harvey." She wrinkled her nose. "If only you'd been this solicitous last night. I'm afraid I learned the hard way about lethal punch."

"Yes...well... That's partly why I'm here. I, of all people, knew you weren't a drinker. You may have noticed I haven't been myself lately. Jeanette made me see how badly I treated you. Will you allow me to apologize?"

Sarah sank onto the couch. "Apologize?" Did he mean he wanted to take up where they'd left off? "Well, Harvey," she said, knowing she couldn't let that impression continue, "things can never be quite the same between us."

"Not even a good working relationship, Sarah?" His face fell. "I'm handing Jeanette's case over to Gordon Banks. Would it help if I told you I never expected to fall in love with a client?"

"Love?" Sarah blinked.

"I do love her, Sarah. Once her case is decided, we're going to be married, whatever the outcome."

"Why, Harvey, I don't know what to say."

"Congratulations was what I'd hoped for," he said, clearing his throat. "She and I have the same goals. The same beliefs. We're a lot alike."

Sarah swallowed her amazement. "Of course, Harvey. I wish you every happiness. I've known for weeks that we had no future together—since the lunch, when it became clear you didn't like Mike."

"I don't dislike the boy. I can't seem to relate to children. My own parents were much older and very strict. As an only child, I was expected to act like an adult. At any rate, you both deserve someone younger. Someone more flexible. Like Gabe Parker. I'd be a terrible father, Sarah. If you want, I'll apologize to Mike, too."

"That won't be necessary. I'll explain. I appreciate your honesty, Harvey. However, I don't want you to have the mistaken impression that there's anything between Gabe and me. You saw me last night in his world—as out of place as you feel in mine."

She heard Mike's door creak. Frowning, she turned to look. Then, because he didn't appear in the hall, she said with some haste, "I don't mean to rush you, Harvey, but I need to see to Mike. He was injured yesterday playing soccer. He's supposed to be confined to bed."

"I'm sorry to hear that."

"Oh, and Harvey...I won't be at work tomorrow. Mitzi's mom is out of town, so I think I'll stay home a few days, instead of looking for a sitter. My work's all caught up. I'll call Lou, of course."

"No problem. I'll tell him. Good legal assistants are worth accommodating." He fidgeted, jingling the change in his pockets.

"Thanks. That's a big load off my mind. I thought about calling a baby-sitting service, but I don't like leaving Mike with a stranger. Goodbye," she said as Harvey opened the door and stepped outside. "Enjoy your brunch."

No sooner had she closed it behind him, bemused by the way some problems seemed to work themselves out while others mushroomed, when Mike spoke in a loud voice. "Gabe's no stranger, Mom. What were you talkin' 'bout? I won't be stayin' with no stranger."

Sarah massaged her temples. "What are you doing out of bed, young man?" As she spun to face him, a sharp pain shot through her head. "Mike, I'm still not feeling a hundred percent. Could we discuss this later?"

"I feel okay," he insisted, with the beginning of a pout. "I don't wanna be sick. I want Gabe to hurry. There's nothin' to do here."

All her child-rearing books said it was wrong to be less than direct with children. They said avoiding issues was dishonest. A great concept, but hard to practice. Then it crossed her mind that if Harvey could clear the air, she should do no less.

"Mike, Harvey gave me next week off. You and I will draw, read and play board games. Won't that be fun? We hardly ever get to do stuff like that. Let's start now. I'll let you watch my TV."

"Don't wanna watch no more TV. Don't want you to stay home. I never do guy things. Fun stuff. I wanna watch surfin'. Gabe promised."

Sarah felt her temper rise. "Gabe is not your father, Mike. He doesn't pay your doctor bills. Nor does he pace the floor at night worrying when you're sick. I'm staying home next week, and that's final. No arguing. The doctor said you should rest." When Mike acted like this she was inclined to throw away her parenting books.

His face contorted and tears loomed. "Mrs. Cline said she thought Gabe was gonna be my new dad. But you won't let him, will you? You don't want us doin' cool stuff. It's all your fault."

"Mike. Honey." Sarah reached out a hand, but he drew back. "Children do not select their own fathers," she said, vexed at the meddling woman. "Mrs. Cline had no right suggesting any such thing."

His tears dripped. The sight of them tore at Sarah's heart. She went to hug him, but again he pulled away. "I know you don't understand, honey. Regular mothers and fathers start by loving each other first. They become parents second. It'll all make sense one day. Please, won't you go lie down?"

"Gabe loves me," he said stubbornly. "I bet he'd love you, too, if you didn't yell at him all the time—like you did last night."

Sarah squared her shoulders. She hadn't realized he'd been awake or that their argument had carried. This was the way Mike had acted before Gabe came on the scene. It was time to do what she should have done before signing up with Befriend an Island Child. Get firm.

"I'm only going to say this once, Mike. Gabe's and my differences have nothing to do with you. He may care a great deal for you, but his responsibilities for your welfare are not the same as mine. I'll give you until I count to three to choose a bed and get in it. Your own or mine. It's up to you."

He whirled and ran toward his room.

"Wait, Mike." Sarah hurried after him. "Don't run. The doctor said to be careful." By the time she reached his door, he'd slammed it, and she could hear him sobbing. She considered following, but how could she explain things any better? Her feelings for Gabe were complex. Sarah didn't fully understand them herself. She decided to let him calm down first. She sighed and checked her watch. Almost two-thirty. Mike had eaten a late breakfast. He'd probably cry himself to sleep and not want anything until dinner.

Surely by then Gabe would call. He wasn't unreasonable. In the cold light of day, he might have come to the same conclusion as she had. Together they'd work something out. Meanwhile she'd let Mike act out his anger and she'd fry chicken, fix potato salad and bake chocolate-chip cookies. His favorites.

Harvey referred to it as bribery, but the experts called it unconditional love. Sarah liked what the books said better. Next week would be special, too: Mike would see. She'd *make* it special.

While the chicken thawed, Sarah downed two cups of strong coffee. Although she felt infinitely better, dark circles still ringed her eyes, she noticed, when she went back to her bedroom to dress and brush her hair and saw her reflection in the mirror.

"Bah." She stuck out her tongue. "No more demon rum for you, lady," she chastened. "Next time, ask what's in those pretty red drinks." Even now, the thought of them puckered her lips. Recalling how uninhibited she'd been brought a flush to her cheeks.

Pushing the memory aside, Sarah pulled on shorts and a sleeveless blouse—appropriate attire for working in a hot kitchen. As she slipped on her sandals, she wondered why it seemed so hard to forget Gabe.

On her way back to the kitchen, she stopped by Mike's door. All was quiet inside except for the garbled murmur of the TV. She tiptoed away, smiling. He would get over his pout, especially once he saw dinner.

Sarah hummed a catchy tune as she gathered ingredients. When she tossed the chocolate-chip bag into the trash and saw the remains of last night's pizza, she remembered Jenny Sue. Mortified, she stopped to call her young sitter's mother—to explain and make arrangements to pay the girl.

Minutes later, Sarah hung up, flustered and deeper in debt to Gabe Parker. Jenny Sue's mother had been all sympathy. *Flu,* she'd said. And Jenny had been generously paid.

Gabe had already covered all bases. No wonder he hadn't called today. He must think her as shallow as a birdbath.

Sarah glanced at the kitchen clock, then threw all her muscle into mixing the thick cookie dough. It was closing on three o'clock. If she hadn't heard from Gabe by six, she'd call him. Her heart leapt erratically, thinking about his voice with its rich cadence, the kind that tied knots in her stomach and sent shivers up her spine.

What if she invited him to dinner? After the times he'd cooked, she owed him. And two adults ought to be able to explain things to one small child.

Without soccer, Gabe's visits would naturally taper off. Sarah found the thought depressing. She hadn't realized how much she'd come to count on him—for Mike's sake. No, she mused, sliding the first pan of cookies into the oven, this was a day for honesty. Despite all their ups and downs, she'd come to count on him for herself. Therein lay the problem.

The clock ticked on as Sarah prepared potato salad and readied the chicken. Four o'clock came and went. She was a little surprised that the smell of cookies hadn't enticed Mike from his room. Except that recently he tended to stay upset longer—particularly when it involved Gabe.

However, she wouldn't let him sulk too long. If he didn't surface by the time the chicken was done, she'd go get him. The delicate part would be skirting her own feelings for Gabe. It would never do to let the child suspect how she felt. He'd have them married off for sure. The thought was appealing. Very appealing...

She smiled and snapped on the radio before dropping cornmeal-coated chicken parts into hot oil. She hummed along with a Beatles tune and was mildly surprised when the radio announcer broke into the middle of it. Sarah caught one word over the sizzle as she dropped the last piece of chicken into the pan. *Tsunami.* Tidal wave. It struck fear into her heart.

Urgently she reached to turn up the radio with her free hand. She shivered, remembering the one and only time she'd lived through a tidal wave—in this very house. She'd been fourteen. It was near the end of monsoon season. Her mother's cancer had taken a turn for the worse and the doctor had her heavily sedated. The woman who stayed during the day had gone, leaving Sarah in charge.

Sarah poked at the pieces of chicken, pulled out those that looked done and placed them on a rack. Friday there had apparently been a submarine quake somewhere off the coast of Mexico that had created a wall of water, which was now rushing toward Hawaii at four hundred miles an hour—growing bigger as it traveled across the sea.

Sweat popped out on Sarah's brow. Her palms grew damp. She rubbed them over her shorts. Last time, the seaquake had developed in the aftermath of an erupting Chilean volcano. Her father had called once from the base to say he was responsible for the navy's aircraft. In his offhand way, he told Sarah she'd be just fine.

In the end, she was. But she would never forget the terror of the hours she'd spent. The sirens—terrifying whooping sounds—sounded unceasingly all night long. Radio and television programs were interrupted frequently, and news broadcasters gave reports in deathlike tones. When all her neighbors began fleeing their homes, suitcases in hand—leaving for higher ground, they said—she had tried unsuccessfully to rouse her mother.

Even now she remembered crying and having no one to hear. She'd vowed then never to marry a man who cared more for airplanes than he did his family. And she hadn't. Sarah smiled bitterly. Farrell Michaels didn't care about airplanes—with him *everything* came before family.

Sarah listened to the reports as she removed the rest of the chicken and turned off the stove. The wave was expected to hit the big island of Hawaii by seven tonight. If it split and didn't run itself out, by seven-thirty Oahu's coastal towns could be in grave danger.

Fortunately her home lay inland. Probably far enough to be safe. Sarah almost had herself convinced and was feeling somewhat better when the announcer mentioned the crazy surfers who were out there trying to catch the swelling waves. The chief of police came on with a stern warning.

Her knees buckled. Gabe's place was right on the beach. Surely he'd had the sense to evacuate. Sarah's heart skipped a beat. Imagine, if she'd given in last night, Mike might well be in danger this very minute!

Suddenly she needed to look in on him.

She hurried down the hall and whisked open his door, expecting to see him asleep or watching TV. His bed was rumpled but empty, the TV blank.

He must have gone to the bathroom. The radio was up too high for her to hear him. Lord, what if he'd fallen?

But no, the bathroom was vacant. Uneasiness sent a surge of acid spiraling into her stomach. *Of course!* She'd offered him her television, which he preferred over his smaller set.

"Mike," she called, opening the door to her room. But her bed was as she'd left it. Sarah gazed around with growing puzzlement. Where could he be? Panic rose, but she fought it down. When he was younger, he often hid from her if he was angry. Although he hadn't pulled that trick in some time, he might have done it now.

But where *was* he? At least her house was small, although it had always been her dream to add on to it someday. Sarah was glad now there were only so many places a boy could hide. He simply must be here someplace.

His walk-in closet was dark. Sarah chewed at the inside of her mouth. What next? All at once, as she scanned the room, she realized the stacks of clothes were no longer on his bed. The clothes and Bear-Bear were gone.

She ran back to the closet and yanked open the door. His carryall—the one he used when he spent late evenings at Mitzi's mom's—wasn't there.

"Lord, no!" Sarah covered her mouth with her hand. He couldn't have... He wouldn't leave the house, would he? If he did, where would he go?

She sat down hard on his bed and gathered his pillow to her chest. A piece of paper floated to the floor. Sarah snatched it up with shaking hands. The message, a childish scrawl, had been written in purple crayon. Most of the words were spelled phonetically. It took a moment for her to decipher: "Gon to see serfin. Dont wury. Gab will tak gud car of me. Luv, Mike."

Tears coursed down Sarah's cheeks and fell in wet blotches on the paper. She jumped up and stuffed the note into a pocket of her shorts. How long had he been gone? Had he called Gabe first?

No. Gabe would never have taken him without telling her. That much she did know. She pulled out the drawer of the nightstand, searching frantically for the phone numbers she knew Gabe had given him. Failing that, she rifled through his treasures. No list. And hers was at the office.

Then she noticed—his piggy bank no longer sat on the chest of drawers. How much money did he have? Was he smart enough to call a cab? Did he know the direction to Sunset Beach? Sarah grabbed her purse and raced for the car. Her fingers shook so much she could barely get the key in the ignition.

How serious was his spleen injury? What would happen if he didn't do exactly as Dr. Manolo said? She turned off the engine and hurried back inside to call the police.

Sergeant Hanna was sympathetic. He also explained they couldn't do much at the moment. Hadn't she heard about the tsunami? Every available officer was working to clear the beaches. He suggested she check with the boy's friends. Nine out of ten children who ran away were found within a block of their own home, he said. Sounding harried, he promised to get on it himself if Mike didn't turn up within the hour.

Only minimally relieved, Sarah hung up. Out she went to cruise the neighborhood. It was five past five. It wouldn't be dark for a while. At each corner, she expected to see him trudging down the sidewalk lugging his carryall. She had her speech prepared. One that wouldn't injure his pride.

After fifteen minutes of driving and suffering disappointment at the homes of his three closest friends, Sarah switched on the radio to chase away the morbidity of her thoughts. At the next stoplight she shut it off again. Reports of the pending tidal wave scared her witless.

The closer she got to the beach highway, the heavier the traffic. Most cars, though, were heading toward town. The absence of tourists on the palm-lined streets was almost eerie. Occasionally a cat or dog streaked out, causing her to brake anxiously, but outside of that sidewalks were vacant.

Would Mike really have tried to go to Sunset Beach?

Yes. The answer hammered in Sarah's now throbbing temples. From experience, she knew there was no way to get Gabe's telephone number. Going to her office would only waste time. She'd ask someone for directions to his beach house.

Turning sharply, she took a shortcut that zigzagged through pineapple fields. Anything to save precious time.

Like it or not, she should listen to the radio. Each update started a new shiver of fear in the pit of her stomach. "Oh, Mike," she cried, as she hit the beach highway. "Be safe, please. Be with Gabe." Never had she prayed so hard for anything in her life.

Dusk was falling when she approached of the first road block.

"What do you think you're doing, lady?" A weary-looking policeman ran up to her car. "You can't go to the beach. We're securing the area. Turn this car around. If you had a lick of sense, you'd find higher ground."

She stared at the lights of the oncoming traffic. "I have to reach Sunset Beach. My son, he's only eight—he's run away." She dug into her pocket and pulled out Mike's note. "Look! I think he's gone there to find a friend who's got a place near where they're holding the surfing trials."

The policeman took the note and studied it. "I'm sorry, ma'am, but I'm afraid there's nothing I can do. I hope they linked up. But I still can't let you through. At last report the wave was five hundred miles off the Big Island. See there—" he pointed "—she's even sucking water from the irrigation ditches out to sea. She won't be stopped at Hawaii, I'm afraid."

As if on cue, the sirens began to howl. Sarah's heart leapt as the noise reverberated in her ears. "You can't stop me," she said between clenched teeth. "What would you do if it was your son?"

His eyes darkened for a moment, but then with a determined look, he stepped in front of her car and physically blocked her path.

Sarah jumped out. "Then I'll walk," she declared, although a mean wind had suddenly sprung up to snatch away her words and her breath.

The young officer grabbed her wrist and fumbled with a set of handcuffs. "I can't let you do that, ma'am. If you won't cooperate, I'll have to detain you by force. Can't you see it's dangerous?"

Sarah had never known such despair. Cars laden with surfboards rode bumper to bumper heading toward town. And Mike was just one small insignificant child.

Gabe! her heart cried, or maybe she called his name aloud. It was now six-fifteen and a tidal wave could kill them all before she had a chance to set things right.

"Mike, oh, Mike, where are you?"

Twisting, Sarah resisted the policeman with every bit of strength she had. Failing to break free, she slumped against the car and buried her face in her hands.

CHAPTER TEN

GABE NOSED HIS WAY into the line of traffic heading toward town from Sunset Beach. He should have gone earlier, right after securing the house. He wanted to leave around three, when Grady Cooper, his general manager at the marina, called to say he'd sent the staff home and was double anchoring the boats. He would have left then if some of those screwball surfers from the mainland hadn't decided it'd be fun to stay and ride *the big one.* Fools, every damn one.

He enjoyed surfing and the thrill of a good ride. But today Sarah's words had left a big impression. Maybe he was ready to roost. She'd been on his mind the entire time he helped clear beaches. Was she worried that he hadn't called? He'd tried once at eleven and her phone had been busy.

Gabe heard the sirens kick in. Damn. It must mean the wave hadn't died at sea. Brother, he hated that incessant shriek. But it could've been worse—like if he'd gone with his first inclination after leaving Sarah and killed that half-bottle of scotch his brother had left at the beach house.

Good thing he'd decided he didn't want the man-size hangover that went with such a juvenile action. He didn't need the guilt, either. He shouldn't have let her get to his ego so easily. What if she or Mike had needed him during the night? Well, he'd know soon.

Gabe glanced at his watch. Holy smoke! How did it get to be so late? Ten past six. Grady would chew his butt for sure. It didn't matter a lick which of them was boss. That old man tended to treat the boat-works as if Grandpa were still alive and he himself still a full partner. Most of the time Gabe didn't object. Those two guys had taught him all they knew about boats. And what they didn't know wasn't worth learning.

At last—the roadblock up ahead in the ocean-bound lane. Not far beyond, the road fanned out into four lanes where traffic moved faster. Drawing close to the blockade, Gabe could see that an officer had a car stopped. The way the fellow was waving his arms it looked like he was having trouble convincing someone to detour. A woman, Gabe noted when he moved another car length. With nice legs, he thought, measuring her shorts with a practiced eye in spite of the gathering dusk. Obviously, though, her elevator didn't run to the top floor. Only a nut would insist on going to the beach with a tsunami on the way.

The Porsche inched ahead as drivers in front of Gabe gawked, too. He was nearly even with the line of barricades before he noticed that the car at the barrier was the same make and color as Sarah's.

Gabe gave the situation a hard look, then did a double take. Hell! It *was* Sarah, and she was crying. Without thinking, he swung out of the slow-moving line and bumped across the shallow ditch dividing the two highways. He yanked on the brake and leapt out before the engine had fully died. "Sarah! What in holy hell are you doing? And where's Mike?"

Startled, Sarah raised her head. "Gabe?" Not believing her eyes, she ran toward him and clutched his shirtfront. "He's not with you? Oh, Gabe!" she cried when he shook his head, dumbfounded. "He's run away."

"Run away? How? Why?"

The officer stepped between them, clearing his throat. "Here's the note, sir. If this woman is a friend, you'd better try talking some sense into her. She insists on going to Sunset Beach."

Sarah tried explaining, but tears choked her words.

Gabe held up a hand. "Wait." Taking the note, he slid his free arm around Sarah's waist as he struggled to read in the dim light.

The policeman snapped on a flashlight, aiming it at the paper.

Gabe crushed the note and stuffed it in his shirt pocket. With two fingers, he gently lifted Sarah's chin. "When did he disappear, sweetheart?" he asked, smoothing her tears away.

There was something about the steady beat of his heart and his even tone that calmed her. "I don't know the actual time. He was mad at me. Because I said he couldn't go with you to the beach. I had decided to stay home next week, and I thought he was sulking." Fresh tears trickled down her cheeks. "He's so little, and he shouldn't even be out of bed. How will I ever find him, Gabe?"

"We'll find him, honey."

His endearments registered only briefly in Sarah's mind. She dismissed them as meaningless. Gabe, too, was worried. She could see it in his eyes. He probably thought sweet nothings were the best way to combat hysteria. Sarah crossed her arms to rub away a sudden chill. "What if someone gave him a ride to the beach after you left?" She wanted to come across as logical, not hysterical.

Gabe turned to the young officer. "How long has the roadblock been up?" he asked.

"Since maybe three o'clock. Give or take ten minutes."

Sarah relaxed. "I know Mike was home at two-thirty. I checked my watch when Harvey left. It was after that Mike and I argued."

"Harvey?" Gabe's jaw tensed. "Did you two make up? That would definitely upset Mike."

"I told you why we had words. It was over you—not Harvey. Mike wanted to spend the week with you."

"Ah, of course, it's all my fault. You know, Sarah, this taking cheap shots at one another isn't getting us anywhere."

"It's not your fault," she corrected. "It's mine."

"Officer?" Gabe beckoned to the policeman now listening on his two-way radio. "Can you use that thing to have someone check my beach house?" Without waiting for an affirmative, Gabe rapped out his address.

In less than five minutes they learned that the beach was cleared and his house locked tight.

"Okay," Gabe said. "Rules that out. We're going to leave the Mustang here and take my car. Any problem with that?"

"No, sir." The cop shook his head. "Just pull her off the road."

Gabe did and handed the keys back to Sarah as he helped her into the Porsche. He nosed his way into the dwindling line of traffic. "Tell me where you've checked." Gabe assumed she must have missed something. Last night Mike could barely walk.

As Sarah told him, Gabe swung from the narrow beach road on to the four-lane highway. Car lights from the opposite lanes lit the Porsche's interior. He glanced over and saw them flicker in a ghostly dance over Sarah's pale cheeks, then gathered her hand in his. It was ice cold.

She clung to his hand as if to a lifeline. "I've never been so frightened," she admitted. "Not even when I was buying the dress for the Maxwell party and some punk pulled a knife on me in the alley. Then I was angry. With this, I feel so helpless."

Gabe arched a brow. "What? Some punk did what?" He sighed. "Someday I want to hear more about that—but not now. Now, we're going to the police."

"I called them. Spoke to Sergeant Hanna. He was nice, but terribly busy." She freed her hand and rubbed her temples. "That shrieking siren gives me the willies. Where could he be, Gabe?" Her voice caught again. "He's never heard the old air-raid sirens. He'll be scared half to death."

"He's tough, Sarah. Think positive. It's a small island."

"Easy for you to say. He's not your son."

"Stop it. If I didn't care, I'd be at my marina making sure my inventory is anchored down. I care about him. And I care about you." *Dammit,* he thought, *let her chew on that for a while.*

She wet her lips and looked away. She couldn't deal with what she heard in his voice—what she saw in his eyes. Not now.

"I'm sorry, Gabe," she said sadly. "You got rather more than you bargained for this time with your agency assignment." A sigh followed. "I owed you before—for last night. I'm not sure I can repay this favor."

"This has nothing to do with the agency, Sarah," Gabe growled. "Ah, good—the police station up ahead. I suggest we get inside before I say something I'll regret, after that last remark." But when they got out, Sarah looked so fragile, so vulnerable, Gabe wished he'd held his tongue.

He paused on the top step and with a steady hand smoothed back her wind-mussed hair. Then he tilted her face and brushed a light kiss over her lips. "For luck," he told her. "We will find him, Sarah. All boys try running away at least once. Neither my brother nor I got very far the time we tried." He opened the heavy door and ushered her toward a uniformed man seated at the front counter.

The desk sergeant looked harried. He had four phones in front of him and all were ringing. But when he tried to mollify them with the same story Sarah had been given over the phone, Gabe demanded to see the captain. They were granted a five-minute audience. Gabe didn't waste words. He gave a concise description of Mike, mentioned his injury and pressured for an all-points bulletin. Sarah was relieved when the captain drummed his fingers on the table a moment, then agreed to an APB.

Gabe jotted down Sarah's number in case the police found Mike while they were still out looking.

"I think we should go recheck your neighborhood, Sarah," he said on the way out. "Bright as Mike is, he's still only eight years old." Privately Gabe agreed with the sergeant. A child's resources were limited at best. Likely, he was closer to home than Sarah thought.

"I searched the house thoroughly. Plus I stopped by the homes of several friends." Sarah's voice sounded strained.

Gabe hustled her along the sidewalk toward the car.

Out on the road, a van went by with a loudspeaker warning people to get off the streets. Apparently the wave was closing on Hawaii, and Oahu's coastline was in imminent danger.

"Damn," Gabe muttered. "I hope Grady managed to tie those boats down without me. This is going to be a doozy."

Sarah grabbed his arm and pulled him up short. "Your boat." Her words tumbled faster. "Maybe he went there. A kid doesn't know one beach from another. What if Mike thought they surfed where you kept your boat?"

Gabe hung back. "I don't know, Sarah. He's pretty smart. He asked a lot of questions about the marina. We can try, but I don't know that the police will let us through."

Sarah looked around at the sky and the street. "It looks so normal." She shivered. "I expected something more dramatic."

"Just wait. It'll get humid and very still right before the wave hits. And you wouldn't want to be near the beach then. The force of those megatons of water does a lot of damage. The last one bent parking meters flat and flooded hotels. But come on, let's give it a shot. If the wave hasn't hit Hawaii yet, they may give us a few minutes to check the marina. If not, I'll call Grady. Nothing much gets by him."

The officer stationed at the barricade on Ala Moana Boulevard was a regular on the harbor beat. He knew Gabe by sight and allowed him ten minutes. The wave had hit the Big Island with horrendous force; it had split as they feared, and now the larger portion was barreling straight for Oahu's leeward beaches. The latest estimated time of arrival was eight o'clock.

Sarah had chewed the inside of her mouth to ribbons. What if this was a wild-goose chase? Where could Mike have gone? Her stomach boiled acid.

"You wait in the car," Gabe instructed as he turned into the Yacht Basin on two wheels and screeched to a stop outside Parker Marina.

"No." Sarah already had her door open. "I'd go crazy waiting. I'm coming."

Gabe took one look at her set lips and didn't argue. "Come on. This way." He unlocked a gate and pulled her inside.

The sirens screamed without any breaks at all now. Gabe unlocked the door to a large white building. "My boat is the one connected to hoists. Why don't you check the cabins and the galley? I'm going into the office to call Grady.

Hurry." He didn't think Mike could have made it this far, but at this point, he dared not rule anything out.

Sarah nodded, crossed her fingers and raced up the ramp. The craft was dark and forbidding. It didn't look promising. Her spirits slid lower with each empty cabin. As she searched, she shouted Mike's name until she was hoarse. When she ran smack into Gabe on the upper deck, he looked grim.

Sarah's heart plummeted. "What is it? What did you find out?" She clutched his arm.

"Let's go. Grady said the roads have been barricaded since two o'clock. Teams have been working since then to evacuate. There's little chance Mike could have slipped through. I think we should go to your house and start again."

"The police..." She sounded hopeful.

"I couldn't get through when I phoned them," he yelled over the wail of sirens as he hustled her outside. "Grady said my mom was the only one who called. Twice. I can't imagine why. But you know mothers," he said, "they never quit worrying." He helped her in and slammed the door. By the time he buckled up, she was fighting tears again.

"Don't, Sarah," he begged. "Crying won't help."

"I—I'm so s-sorry," she stammered, but she couldn't seem to stop.

He let out a pent-up breath, drove past the barrier and down a block, then pulled over to the curb and took her into his arms. "Shh," he whispered, threading his fingers through her tumbled hair. He rocked her gently, as he might have rocked Mike, and crooned nonsense into her ear.

"It's all m-my f-fault." Sarah scrubbed at the tears. "I've b-been denying the s-signs. All the books are clear."

"Your parenting books?" He cupped her face and brushed his thumbs over her cheeks.

"Yes. It's called transference. Mike wanted a father so bad, he—" She bit her lip and sucked in air. "I'm afraid he placed you in that role. I should have discussed it with you, but I had these feelings of my own that kept getting in the way. I was wrong, and now look. He's gone to f-find you, and you're needed at h-home. I don't know what to do."

Gabe bent and kissed her quiet. Then he drew back and drove away from the curb. "You've been in denial over a lot of things, Sarah," he said calmly. "But there'll be time for us to clear the air later. Right now we're going to *your* house. Have faith in Mike's intelligence, Sarah. He knows what Dr. Manolo said. I can't help thinking he's all right. I feel it in my bones."

Sarah laced her fingers tightly together. Her mind was a chaotic jumble. According to Mike, Gabe always knew best. At this moment, she wanted with all her heart to trust that he did.

Leaning back, she tried to block the sirens and collect her thoughts. If Gabe hadn't found her, what then? Mike was her responsibility. It was about time she stopped acting helpless.

As they turned into her driveway, she was outwardly as calm as Gabe. The old Sarah. Cool. Efficient. No one but Gabe would know the fears that lay underneath.

The house was dark and empty. Gabe turned on the lights and went straight to Sarah's answering machine. It wasn't on. He swore to himself; he'd given this number to the sergeant. Plus, if Mike was lost and confused, he might have tried calling. For Sarah's sake, he hid his concern.

But Sarah saw. "I must have fiddled with it accidentally when I talked with the police. I can't believe I did that." She looked stricken.

"What about Mitzi and Osamu?" Gabe asked. "Would Mike go there?"

She shook her head. "Mitzi and her mom are out of town. And Osamu's is wise to the ways of kids. He would have brought him home."

Gabe rang the police again. It took three tries to get through. They hadn't found Mike, but neither had they turned up any unidentified bodies. Gabe didn't think he'd tell Sarah that part. She was back searching rooms.

He knew from the shadows in her eyes when she rejoined him that nothing new had turned up. He pulled her into his arms and held her close.

"I hoped I'd find him asleep in one of the closets. When he was three or four, he'd hide there when he got mad at me. I remember how it troubled me, until I read in one of the books that it was fairly common for his age. But now..." She stopped and lifted a determined jaw. "I'm going to call everyone in his class. It's a small neighborhood. Maybe someone saw him."

Gabe nodded. "That's the spirit. I'll take a run up to the school. It's possible he was more upset than we thought about having to give up soccer."

"Shouldn't you try your mother?" Sarah asked. "You said that man Grady mentioned she's called twice."

"We'll do this first. When I come back, if you've finished making your calls, I'll give her a jingle. Whatever she needs, she has infinitely more people to help her than you do. More than likely she got upset when she wasn't able to reach me at the beach house. She's kind of like you." He dropped a light kiss on Sarah's nose.

Sarah didn't say anything. His generosity overwhelmed her. Mike's real father had never been a fraction this benevolent, this caring.

Gabe had his hand on the doorknob when Sarah knew she had to tell him the truth. If nothing else, he deserved to know why she hated everything to do with surfing. She grabbed his arm. "One Sunday," she said without preamble, "Mike had chicken pox. His fever went sky-high. I'd walked the floor with him for three days and nights. I was exhausted, and Farrell took off for Makaha to surf. He had the checkbook, the teller card and the last of our cash. I couldn't even buy juice. I think I went a little crazy. Anyway, I wrapped Mike up and drove to the beach...to beg, if I had to, for help."

Tears trickled down her cheeks and Gabe came back and kissed them away. "Honey, don't. It's okay. Don't torture yourself."

"I want you to know why I hate surfing. Surfers," she whispered. "I found my husband, all right. He was in the middle of a big party. I explained what I needed and he popped the top on another beer. Then he slid his arm around some blonde in a string bikini and reminded me that I was the one who wanted a baby."

"Oh, sweetheart," he said. "I'll never bring up surfing again. I swear. If I'd been there, I'd have thrashed him. How did you manage?"

"I took Mike to the emergency room. They admitted him because they were worried about meningitis. The moment he recovered, I called Lou and asked him to file for a divorce. Unfortunately Farrell got wind of this, or he guessed. At any rate, he cleaned out our checking and savings and left Hawaii before Lou could have the papers served. Then he filed first—from Australia."

Slipping from Gabe's arms, Sarah picked up the phone. "Everything you've done—are doing—means a lot to me. I just wanted you to know."

He shook his head, looking sober. "I only wish I'd known before. Maybe we wouldn't be in this mess now. I promise you, Sarah, when this is over, when we find Mike, we have things to discuss." With that, he was gone.

The tsunami hit Oahu while Sarah was on the telephone with Mrs. Cline. The Clines had their television turned up loud to drown out the sirens. The report came while the woman went to ask Jim if he'd seen Mike today. Eighty-foot swells had ripped through beachfront hotels. Power had failed and miles of coastline were blacked out. Waikiki, where Gabe's marina lay, was receiving the brunt of the impact. Sarah prayed he hadn't been wiped out and that they hadn't missed something in their quick search. She refused to think what it would mean if Mike had made his way to the beach.

Her faith weakened a bit when Jim Cline said he'd been out playing all day and had seen nothing. Sarah's hands shook as she dialed the next number. It was the same story. No one had seen him. It was as if he'd vanished without a trace.

She had just dialed the last child in Mike's class when Gabe returned. She could tell by the look on his face that he'd met dead ends, too. She tried not to react, but felt her shoulders slump in defeat.

Gabe walked over and, as Sarah wound down her conversation with Benny Olani's mother, began massaging her neck. But there was no hope there, either; Benny hadn't seen Mike.

The receiver fell from Sarah's hand. As he knelt to pick it up, the terror in her dark eyes ripped a hole in his heart. "Why don't you go make coffee?" he suggested quietly. "I'll give the police captain another try. They may have tried to call while you were on the phone."

She nodded. "And don't forget your mother." Putting on a brave front, she moved toward the kitchen. "I'm sorry about your marina, Gabe. I heard on the Clines' TV that Waikiki was hit hard."

"Insignificant compared to Mike, Sarah. Go on. Let me make this call." He made numerous tries before he got through. Gabe stared into space as he listened. The police had nothing. Furthermore, now that the wave had hit, the entire force would be pressed into duty to keep looters out of the hotels and businesses that had been flooded.

"I understand," Gabe said wearily. "I hate even to suggest this, but would you ask your officers to keep an eye out during cleanup?" The captain said he would, and Gabe hung up.

He stood and stretched his own tense muscles before calling his mother. Gabe felt as if he'd aged ten years. He could only guess at the turmoil Sarah must be battling. Sinking down on the couch, he pulled the phone to his lap and halfheartedly dialed his parents' home.

"Hi, Mom. It's Gabe. Grady said you called. What's up?" He listened for a moment, then straightened. "What?" he yelled. Jumping up, he covered the mouthpiece and shouted for Sarah.

She appeared in the kitchen doorway, her red-rimmed eyes dark and wary. "Tell me," she rasped. "Have the police found something?"

He smiled and motioned her forward. "Not the police. My mother." His voice rose in excitement. "Near as I can understand, Mike got mixed up on the numbers I gave him and called my parents, instead of me. She told him to stay by the pay phone and that she'd come get him. Once she heard his story—how he was mad at you and running away—she promised to locate me. When she couldn't find me anywhere, she talked him into trying you. But by then, you must have been out looking. She never got through to the police. She's been in a tizzy, knowing how frantic you must be."

He reached for Sarah and dropped a happy kiss on the top of her head. "Do you want to talk to him on the phone, or should we turn off that coffee and make tracks over there?"

"Oh, yes, let's just go," she said, covering her mouth with both hands. "Right after you phone the captain and tell him Mike's been found." This time, the tears pouring down her cheeks were tears of joy.

"I can't believe it," she said for about the fiftieth time as they took a circuitous route around roadblocks to an exclusive region of homes on the cliffs overlooking Diamond Head. "Why didn't she just bring him home?"

Gabe squeezed her knee. "Are you kidding? After her escapades with two rambunctious boys, she probably figured he'd just try something later. That's only a guess, mind you."

Sarah glanced at him and smiled. "I thought you said you only tried running away once."

He looked abashed. "Uh, did I say that?"

She laughed, then threw up her hands. "Do you know how good it feels to laugh? I didn't think I ever would again."

He traced a finger down her nose and over her lips. "You don't laugh enough. Marry me, and I'll guarantee you a lifetime filled with love and laughter." Totally unrehearsed, the words had just seemed to tumble out.

Sarah gaped. She sat very straight and folded her hands tightly in her lap, hardly daring to breathe. It was foolish. And crazy. And so tempting.

"Don't answer now if you're going to say no," he said urgently. "I realize my timing is lousy. I'd intended to bombard you with candy and flowers and then offer you all the right words and a ring during a romantic dinner for two." He shrugged repentantly. "Heck of a thing, a guy telling you he loves you when all your defenses are down." Gabe knew he was rambling, but she'd gone so still it scared the hell out of him. He watched her carefully.

Sarah placed a hand on his stubbled cheek. She couldn't help thinking, again, how much he looked like Mike. "Are you sure you're not just caught up in the moment, Gabe? I know you've been alarmed for Mike. We've shared quite a dramatic few hours."

He turned his face and kissed her palm. "If we weren't parked in front of my parents' gate—and if my mother, bless her heart, wasn't viewing this whole scene on her security monitor—I'd show you dramatic. X-rated. It's markedly different from what I feel for your son, Mrs. Michaels."

She blinked as the gates swung inward and tried to escape the red eye of the sensor. "Oh, Lord. What must she be thinking about my touching you like this? I mean, we know how your sister-in-law feels about me."

Grinning, Gabe parked behind a midnight-blue Rolls blocking the circular drive. His father's car. Wonder of wonders—the old man was home. "Don't think Mother's like Mariel. Basically she's old-fashioned. She'll probably ask what your intentions are toward her poor innocent son." He laughed, then swallowed it as Sarah got a look at Billings, the butler who'd run the Parker home since before Gabe was born—and was now striding purposefully down the marble steps to help Sarah from the car. At six foot five, and three hundred pounds, he resembled a tank in a tux.

Her eyes were wide. Stunned.

It amused Gabe to see her give a smart tug on her shorts and smooth a nervous hand over her hair.

"Billings, you're spooking the lady. And don't you dare tell her any stories about my wild youth. Skip right to what a nice guy I am."

"Ah. Is this our young visitor's mother?" The big man's smile grew. He offered Sarah his arm and patted her hand, saying conspiratorially, "That boy of yours reminds me of Gabriel at the same age. Except that your son has better manners."

Gabe sputtered, and it was Sarah's turn to laugh outright.

"I can tell you don't really know him," she said. "Those are his company manners. I suspect he's more like Gabe than you know. In fact, he's given us quite a fright today. Is he all right? I thought for sure he'd come out to meet us."

Gabe fell back a pace, pleased to see that Sarah had gotten over the first shock of seeing his parents' opulent home. He'd have to tell her it was *their* style, not his. And he'd have to tell the family that he was leaving the hotel business for good. The marina provided more than enough income to support a family.

But when Billings ushered them into the den, the sight greeting him drove everything else from Gabe's mind. His father—the hard-driving, gruff-talking billionaire—was stretched out on his fifty-thousand dollar Aubusson rug playing chess with Sarah's son. Gabe was struck speechless. He'd lost count of all the times, as a boy, he'd asked his father to play and been turned down because his dad was too busy.

Mike looked up and waved. "Hi, Mom. Hi, Gabe. Grampa Dave is teachin' me how to play chest. It's compelcated, but he thinks I'm doin' real good."

"Complicated," Sarah and Gabe said together. Surprised, they turned and looked at one another just as they both said "chess" in wondering tones.

"Mike," Sarah chided when she'd stopped laughing, "we've been worried sick about you. Don't we rate more than a casual hi? And who gave you permission to call Gabe's father anything but Mr. Parker?"

"Um, I did." Flushing, the elder Parker scrambled to his feet. He studied Sarah through eyes very like Gabe's in color and clarity before turning to look helplessly at his wife, who'd just come in. "Didn't you tell me Gabe was gonna marry this lady?" he muttered in a gruff voice.

Nonplussed, the attractive older woman, half his size, slipped her arm through his. "Well, David," she scolded gently, "I'm afraid you may have precipitated his asking."

Gabe didn't let his father dangle in the noose of his own making for too long, although he was tempted—seeing as it was the first time he'd seen the old man at a loss for words. "Relax, Pop. I already asked her. She just hasn't given me an answer. Yet." He tugged at one ear. "I don't suppose she can hear the question too many times, though."

He crossed the room and knelt beside Mike. "It might help my case if you promised not to pull a stunt like this again, kicker. You really gave us a bad scare."

Mike lowered his eyes. "I'm sorry. I was scared, too. The sirens... And they showed all that stuff on TV 'bout the waves that hit here before. I was real scared for my mom, 'specially after Gramma Charlotte said she wasn't home." Suddenly a confident grin edged out his frown. "Grampa Dave said you were too smart to let the tidal wave get you. I shoulda known you'd take care of Mom." Getting awkwardly to his feet, he ran across the room and flung his arms around his mother's waist. "I won't ever do nothin' like that again. I promise."

Gabe and his father locked eyes a moment, then they both turned to watch mother and child. David Parker's hand came out to rest lightly on his son's shoulder.

"Thanks for the vote of confidence, Dad," Gabe said with feeling. "All these years...I've never known what you thought."

"Yes, well, I never doubted your ability to survive. You're a lot like my father in that respect." The older man tipped his silvery head toward Mike. "That boy's stubborn, too. I hope you plan to spend some time with him. Don't make the same mistakes I did. I've regretted it more than you know. So many years—they just seemed to get away."

"Dad." Gabe's voice cracked. He brushed one thumb over his stubbled jaw, regained his composure and said with some hesitation, "Sarah hasn't agreed to marry me. Don't steamroll her." He shot her an anxious look then, aware that he hadn't exactly trodden too softly himself.

Embarrassed at being the object of their conversation, Sarah combed nervous fingers through Mike's golden curls until he ducked away from her hand.

Gabe's mother offered her a sympathetic smile. "I doubt anyone here has eaten much today," she said. "We tried feeding Mike, but I think he was too troubled by what he'd done to eat. Could I interest anyone in fried chicken, potato salad and chocolate-chip cookies?"

"Oh, boy! Oh, boy!" Mike hopped around, begging to stay.

Sarah told him to settle down, then said, "Why, that's Mike's favorite dinner. In fact, I was making the very same thing at home before all this happened."

"Really?" Gabe's mother arched a brow. "Funny. It's David's and Gabe's favorite, too."

Mike grabbed Sarah's hand, then reached for Gabe's. Peeking slyly at one, then the other, he said as if it was a matter of course, "If you guys got married, we could take one of them honeymooms on Gabe's boat—like I seen once on TV. Mom can bring her fried chicken, potato salad and cookies. Gabe and me'll drive the boat."

"Sail the boat, kicker," Gabe said. "And the word is honey*moon*. But kids don't go."

"They don't?" Mike's face fell.

"No," Sarah said. "No kids allowed. The honeymoon is just for Gabe and me."

Gabe threw her a glance, his heart climbing into his throat. Did that mean . . . ? He waited impatiently for her to elaborate.

Mike stepped back to stand beside Gabe's father. "Boy, Grampa Dave," he said with a sigh. "I didn't think Mom'd ever say she'd go. Now can I stay here and learn more about chest like me and you planned?"

"Chess," the elder Parker corrected, grinning broadly. "And yes, you may."

"Mike!" Sarah was horrified until she noticed that all three Parkers were trying to suppress smiles. "Oh, I give up.'' She joined the laughter with an overwhelming sense of relief. She knew now that Gabe's *real* world was no different from her own—knew that the same things mattered to both of them. She knew it with a certainty that reached to the bottom of her heart....

Gabe wrapped her in a bear hug and gave her a long leisurely kiss. When at last he let her go, he muttered, ''I'd feel a whole lot better if you mentioned somewhere in here that you loved me.''

Gabe's parents each snatched one of Mike's hands and hustled him toward the door. He wiggled loose and craned his neck. ''What you doin', Gabe? Teachin Mom to kiss?''

Sarah's face flamed.

''Nope,'' Gabe answered. ''She does that pretty well now.''

''Oh!'' Mike trudged after Gabe's parents. At the door he turned again. ''Aunt Mitzi said someone hadda show her how to hang loose. I'm kinda countin' on you, Gabe. Else I ain't never gonna get to see 'em surf.''

''After the doctor says you're well,'' Sarah promised, although she didn't even scold him for saying ''ain't.'' She smiled up into Gabe's eyes. If that last tidbit wasn't proof of her love, after all the times she'd said no to surfing, she didn't know what was.

''All right!'' Mike yelped, starting to skip. Then he stopped as if he'd thought better of it and walked sedately through the archway.

Gabe held his tongue until they seemed to be alone. Sliding his arms down Sarah's back, he molded her body tightly to his. ''Is that what this is about?'' he growled. ''Banishing ex-husbands and surfing phobias, Sarah?'' It had better not be, his look warned. He was just old-fashioned enough to want the words.

She shook her head. ''It's about love—and about me trusting you enough to hang loose.'' Sarah brushed a finger over the deep crease caused by his sudden grin. ''Don't you recognize the change?''

''How loose is loose?'' he murmured, dropping a row of kisses from her ear to the pulse hammering in her throat.

"Oh, Gabe," she breathed, "you talk in riddles, just like Mike. From the moment our paths crossed, you two were so much alike it was scary. One more reason I can't help loving you," she mused, following his lips for a kiss.

"At last!" he exclaimed, leaning back triumphantly. "Those little words I've been waiting to hear."

"Zowie!" Mike yelled, withdrawing his nose from around the corner of the door casing. "Mom finally said she loves him. Let's eat, guys."

Gabe threw back his head and laughed. "A man after my own heart."

Sarah punched his arm. "I'll race you to the table."

"Hey," Gabe called. "You've got a head start."

When he rounded the corner after her, Sarah leapt out, threw her arms around his neck and smothered his lips in a kiss more ardent than the one he'd bestowed on her. "Is that loose enough to take your mind off food, Parker?" she asked, suddenly breathless.

He groaned. "If you hang much looser, lady, I can almost guarantee the honeymoom, as our son calls it, will precede the wedding. As it is, I'm considering letting Grady assess the marina damage all by his lonesome."

At the words "our son," Sarah's heart filled to bursting. They were going to be a family. She and Mike and Gabe.

And wouldn't Mitzi be furious—missing the news of the decade? Smiling, Sarah rose on tiptoe and claimed another lengthy kiss.

Gabe didn't quite know how to break it to those waiting in the kitchen. But kissing Sarah beat fried chicken, potato salad—and even chocolate-chip cookies.

EPILOGUE

"HURRY UP, will you, Dad? Mom'll be hoppin' up and down, and she'll say it's my fault we're late." Mike gave the cocker spaniel Gabe's father had given him for his tenth birthday a final pat and shut the gate.

Gabe unlocked the minivan he'd bought to pick up Sarah and his new offspring from the hospital, pausing to ruffle the slicked-down curls of his adopted son. Mike, he thought, was growing more like him every day. Patience wasn't *his* long suit, either.

The youngster, trying to act like a grown-up ten, pulled out his comb and juggled gaily wrapped packages while he attempted to flatten his curls again.

It seemed to Gabe that Mike had sprouted a foot since Lou Page had tracked down Farrell Michaels and got him to sign the adoption papers.

"Mom don't like surprises," the boy said as he climbed into the van and buckled in.

"Doesn't," Gabe corrected. It had become second nature to him. "But to which surprise are you referring? She's had a few lately."

"That nanny Gramma Charlotte sent. The mess you and Grampa Dave made addin' bedrooms was bad 'nuff. A nanny'll send her into orbit. You sure Mom'll like my presents?" he asked before Gabe could mention the *g*'s he'd dropped.

"What's not to like?" Gabe asked, backing over the newly asphalted drive onto the main street. "They're frilly."

Mike leaned over Gabe's shoulder. "Jim Cline said babies are a lot like puppies. They sleep and eat. Is that true?"

Gabe laughed. If he had a dollar for every time over the past year and a half that Mike had demanded to know if something was true, he'd be a rich man. "True enough, son," he concurred. "Plus, they wet."

"Oh." Mike sat back, looking thoughtful. "Is that 'cause they're girls? Girls are always runnin' to the bathroom when we chase 'em at recess," he said wisely.

This time Gabe swallowed his grin. "Now *that* will surprise your mother, kicker. She says her books don't have nearly enough about infatuation."

"'Fatuation?" The boy wrinkled his nose. "Susan Dixon isn't fat. She's pretty. She has long red hair. Don'cha 'member? Susan was at soccer camp this summer. She plays soccer real good."

"Susan?" Gabe glanced sharply in the rearview mirror. "I see. That's why you chose the name for your sister so readily. Sue the soccer ace."

Mike blushed. "You said Mom liked the name."

"She does. Her only stipulation was nothing cutesy, like DeeDee or Sheena. Hey, here we are, kicker. St. Jude's. Are you ready for this?"

"Sure. Feed 'em. Burp 'em. Rock 'em. It's cool."

"Ye-e-es," Gabe drawled as they got out. "More or less. Why don't you wait in the lobby? Your mother promised to be ready."

"Hurry up. I feel dumb holdin' *pink* packages. What if one of the guys sees me?"

"Give them one of the lollipops that say 'It's a girl!' "

Sarah was ready when Gabe stepped into her room. He kissed her hello and said how beautiful she was as he helped her into the wheelchair—a requisite for new mothers. Then he kissed his babies. "Mike's downstairs. He bought presents all by himself with his lawn-mowing money. You'll be glad to hear I steered him away from the hot-pink and chartreuse soccer balls."

"Will he be jealous, do you think?" Sarah asked worriedly, reaching for Gabe's hand as the elevator began its descent. He glanced over at the nurses who were carrying his daughters and rolled his eyes. "I think we'll keep him too busy for that, love."

The elevator door slid open, and Mike spotted them at once. He stood as they approached. Packages fell at his feet. "Wow," he said, frankly awed. "I know Dad said we had triples, but I didn't know they'd all look alike."

"*Triplets,*" Sarah corrected, moving to hug him. "Abigail, Emily and Susan, meet your big brother, Mike." She indicated three rosebud faces, all sound asleep. Before she could say more, the outer doors opened and Mitzi and Osamu rushed in carrying three large pink panda bears, followed closely by Gabe's parents, who clutched three dolls.

A very pregnant Mitzi stopped short and flashed Sarah a big grin, along with the island hang-loose sign. "I've never seen you looking so content, my friend," she said, "but see if I ever advise you to hang loose again."

Osamu stepped up, shook Gabe's hand and tweaked Sarah's nose. Yet it was at Mike that he winked and said solemnly, "I swear this wasn't in the plan when I recommended Befriend an Island Child to your mother. I'm still in a fog over the prospect of one baby. And you have three."

"I know, Sam," said Mike. "Ain't I the luckiest kid on Oahu?"

"*Ain't,* Mike!" a chorus of adults scolded.

The boy shot them a long-suffering look and picked up his three pink packages. "I think we should go home and get busy feedin' and burpin' these triples, so you guys won't have so much time to fuss about the way I talk. That's what I think."

Gabe slid an arm around Sarah. "We'll work on *g*'s this winter."

"Hang loose, Gabriel," she said, smiling softly. "We've got a few years before he hits college. That new book you bought promises he'll outgrow it."

"Oh, brother." Mike rolled his eyes. "You guys and your dumb books! Good thing these triples got *me* around to tell 'em stuff."

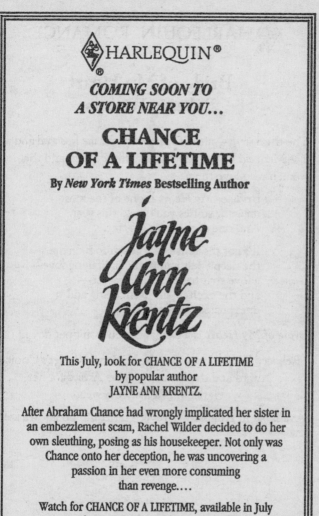

INDULGE A LITTLE 6947 SWEEPSTAKES
NO PURCHASE NECESSARY

HERE'S HOW THE SWEEPSTAKES WORKS:
The Harlequin Reader Service shipments for January, February and March 1994 will contain, respectively, coupons for entry into three prize drawings: a trip for two to San Francisco, an Alaskan cruise for two and a trip for two to Hawaii. To be eligible for any drawing using an Entry Coupon, simply complete and mail according to directions.

There is no obligation to continue as a Reader Service subscriber to enter and be eligible for any prize drawing. You may also enter any drawing by hand printing your name and address on a 3" x 5" card and the destination of the prize you wish that entry to be considered for (i.e., San Francisco trip, Alaskan cruise or Hawaiian trip). Send your 3" x 5" entries to: Indulge a Little 6947 Sweepstakes, c/o Prize Destination you wish that entry to be considered for, P.O. Box 1315, Buffalo, NY 14269-1315, U.S.A. or Indulge a Little 6947 Sweepstakes, P.O. Box 610, Fort Erie, Ontario L2A 5X3, Canada.

To be eligible for the San Francisco trip, entries must be received by 4/30/94; for the Alaskan cruise, 5/31/94; and the Hawaiian trip, 6/30/94. No responsibility is assumed for lost, late or misdirected mail. Sweepstakes open to residents of the U.S. (except Puerto Rico) and Canada, 18 years of age or older. All applicable laws and regulations apply. Sweepstakes void wherever prohibited.

For a copy of the Official Rules, send a self-addressed, stamped envelope (WA residents need not affix return postage) to: Indulge a Little 6947 Rules, P.O. Box 4631, Blair, NE 68009, U.S.A.

INDR93

INDULGE A LITTLE 6947 SWEEPSTAKES
NO PURCHASE NECESSARY

HERE'S HOW THE SWEEPSTAKES WORKS:
The Harlequin Reader Service shipments for January, February and March 1994 will contain, respectively, coupons for entry into three prize drawings: a trip for two to San Francisco, an Alaskan cruise for two and a trip for two to Hawaii. To be eligible for any drawing using an Entry Coupon, simply complete and mail according to directions.

There is no obligation to continue as a Reader Service subscriber to enter and be eligible for any prize drawing. You may also enter any drawing by hand printing your name and address on a 3" x 5" card and the destination of the prize you wish that entry to be considered for (i.e., San Francisco trip, Alaskan cruise or Hawaiian trip). Send your 3" x 5" entries to: Indulge a Little 6947 Sweepstakes, c/o Prize Destination you wish that entry to be considered for, P.O. Box 1315, Buffalo, NY 14269-1315, U.S.A. or Indulge a Little 6947 Sweepstakes, P.O. Box 610, Fort Erie, Ontario L2A 5X3, Canada.

To be eligible for the San Francisco trip, entries must be received by 4/30/94; for the Alaskan cruise, 5/31/94; and the Hawaiian trip, 6/30/94. No responsibility is assumed for lost, late or misdirected mail. Sweepstakes open to residents of the U.S. (except Puerto Rico) and Canada, 18 years of age or older. All applicable laws and regulations apply. Sweepstakes void wherever prohibited.

For a copy of the Official Rules, send a self-addressed, stamped envelope (WA residents need not affix return postage) to: Indulge a Little 6947 Rules, P.O. Box 4631, Blair, NE 68009, U.S.A.

INDR93

INDULGE A LITTLE
SWEEPSTAKES

OFFICIAL ENTRY COUPON

This entry must be received by: JUNE 30, 1994
This month's winner will be notified by: JULY 15, 1994
Trip must be taken between: AUGUST 31, 1994-AUGUST 31, 1995

YES, I want to win the 3-Island Hawaiian vacation for two. I understand that the prize includes round-trip airfare, first-class hotels and pocket money as revealed on the "wallet" scratch-off card.

Name____

Address __________________________ Apt. ____________

City____

State/Prov.__________________ Zip/Postal Code____________

Daytime phone number____________________________
(Area Code)

Account #____________________________________

Return entries with invoice in envelope provided. Each book in this shipment has two entry coupons—and the more coupons you enter, the better your chances of winning!

 MONTH3

INDULGE A LITTLE
SWEEPSTAKES

OFFICIAL ENTRY COUPON

This entry must be received by: JUNE 30, 1994
This month's winner will be notified by: JULY 15, 1994
Trip must be taken between: AUGUST 31, 1994-AUGUST 31, 1995

YES, I want to win the 3-Island Hawaiian vacation for two. I understand that the prize includes round-trip airfare, first-class hotels and pocket money as revealed on the "wallet" scratch-off card.

Name____

Address __________________________ Apt. ____________

City____

State/Prov.__________________ Zip/Postal Code____________

Daytime phone number____________________________
(Area Code)

Account #____________________________________

Return entries with invoice in envelope provided. Each book in this shipment has two entry coupons—and the more coupons you enter, the better your chances of winning!

© 1993 HARLEQUIN ENTERPRISES LTD. MONTH3